The Indiscretion of the Duchess

Autor

Contents

THE INDISCRETION OF THE DUCHESS

BY

Autor

CHAPTER I.
A Multitude of Good Reasons.

In accordance with many most excellent precedents, I might begin by claiming the sympathy due to an orphan alone in the world. I might even summon my unguided childhood and the absence of parental training to excuse my faults and extenuate my indiscretions. But the sympathy which I should thus gain would be achieved, I fear, by something very like false pretenses. For my solitary state sat very lightly upon me--the sad events which caused it being softened by the influence of time and habit--and had the recommendation of leaving me, not only free to manage my own life as I pleased, but also possessed of a competence which added power to my freedom. And as to the indiscretions--well, to speak it in all modesty and with a becoming consciousness of human frailty, I think that the undoubted indiscretions--that I may use no harder term--which were committed in the course of a certain fortnight were not for the most part of my doing or contriving. For throughout the transactions which followed on my arrival in France, I was rather the sport of circumstances than the originator of any scheme; and the prominent part which I played was forced upon me, at first by whimsical chance, and later on by the imperious calls made upon me by the position into which I was thrust.

The same reason that absolves me from the need of excuse deprives me of the claim to praise; and, looking back, I am content to find nothing of which I need seriously be ashamed, and glad to acknowledge that, although Fate chose to put me through some queer paces, she was not in the end malevolent, and that, now the whole thing is finished, I have no cause to complain of the ultimate outcome of it. In saying that, I speak purely and solely for myself. There is one other for whom I might perhaps venture to say the same without undue presumption, but I will not;

while for the rest, it must suffice for me to record their fortunes, without entering on the deep and grave questions which are apt to suggest themselves to anyone who considers with a thoughtful mind the characters and the lives of those with whom he is brought in contact on his way through the world. The good in wicked folk, the depths in shallow folk, the designs of haphazard minds, the impulsive follies of the cunning--all these exist, to be dimly discerned by any one of us, to be ignored by none save those who are content to label a man with the name of one quality and ignore all else in him, but to be traced, fully understood, and intelligently shown forth only by the few who are gifted to read and expound the secrets of human hearts. That is a gift beyond my endowment, and fitted for a task too difficult for my hand. Frankly, I did not, always and throughout, discern as clearly as I could desire the springs on which the conduct of my fellow-actors turned; and the account I have given of their feelings and their motives must be accepted merely as my reading of them, and for what, as such, it is worth. The actual facts speak for themselves. Let each man read them as he will; and if he does not indorse all my views, yet he will, I venture to think, be recompensed by a story which even the greatest familiarity and long pondering has not robbed of all its interest for me. But then I must admit that I have reasons which no one else can have for following with avidity every stage and every development in the drama, and for seeking to discern now what at the time was dark and puzzling to me.

The thing began in the most ordinary way in the world--or perhaps that is too strongly put. The beginning was ordinary indeed, and tame, compared with the sequel. Yet even the beginning had a flavor of the unusual about it, strong enough to startle a man so used to a humdrum life and so unversed in anything out of the common as I. Here, then, is the beginning:

One morning, as I sat smoking my after-breakfast cigar in my rooms in St. James' Street, my friend Gustave de Berensac rushed in. His bright brown eyes were sparkling, his mustache seemed twisted up more gayly and triumphantly than ever, and his manner was redolent of high spirits. Yet it was a dull, somber, misty morning, for all that the month was July and another day or two would bring August. But Gustave was a merry fellow, though always (as I had occasion to remember later on) within the limits of becoming mirth--as to which, to be sure, there may be much difference of opinion.

"Shame!" he cried, pointing at me. "You are a man of leisure, nothing keeps you here; yet you stay in this **bouillon** of an atmosphere, with France only twenty miles away over the sea!"

"They have fogs in France too," said I. "But whither tends your impassioned speech, my good friend? Have you got leave?"

Gustave was at this time an extra secretary at the French Embassy in London.

"Leave? Yes, I have leave--and, what is more, I have a charming invitation."

"My congratulations," said I.

"An invitation which includes a friend," he continued, sitting down. "Ah, you smile! You mean that is less interesting?"

"A man may smile and smile, and not be a villain," said I. "I meant nothing of the sort. I smiled at your exhilaration--nothing more, on the word of a moral Englishman."

Gustave grimaced; then he waved his cigarette in the air, exclaiming:

"She is charming, my dear Gilbert!"

"The exhilaration is explained."

"There is not a word to be said against her," he added hastily.

"That does not depress me," said I. "But why should she invite me?"

"She doesn't invite you; she invites me to bring--anybody!"

"Then she is ennuyée, I presume?"

"Who would not be, placed as she is? He is inhuman!"

"M. le mari?"

"You are not so stupid, after all! He forbids her to see a single soul; we must steal our visit, if we go."

"He is away, then?"

"The kind government has sent him on a special mission of inquiry to Algeria. Three cheers for the government!"

"By all means," said I. "When are you going to approach the subject of who these people are?"

"You will not trust my discernment?"

"Alas, no! You are too charitable--to one half of humanity."

"Well, I will tell you. She is a great friend of my sister's--they were brought up in the same convent; she is also a good comrade of mine."

"A good comrade?"

"That is just it; for I, you know, suffer hopelessly elsewhere."

"What, Lady Cynthia still?"

"Still!" echoed Gustave with a tragic air. But he recovered in a moment. "Lady Cynthia being, however, in Switzerland, there is no reason why I should not go to Normandy."

"Oh, Normandy?"

"Precisely. It is there that the duchess--"

"Oho! The duchess?"

"Is residing in retirement in a small château, alone save for my sister's society."

"And a servant or two, I presume?"

"You are just right, a servant or two; for he is most stingy to her (though not, they say, to everybody), and gives her nothing when he is away."

"Money is a temptation, you see."

"Mon Dieu, to have none is a greater!" and Gustave shook his head solemnly.

"The duchess of what?" I asked patiently.

"You will have heard of her," he said, with a proud smile. Evidently he thought that the lady was a trump card. "The Duchess of Saint-Maclou."

I laid down my cigar, maintaining, however, a calm demeanor.

"Aha!" said Gustave. "You will come, my friend?"

I could not deny that Gustave had a right to his little triumph; for a year ago, when the duchess had visited England with her husband, I had received an invitation to meet her at the Embassy. Unhappily, the death of a relative (whom I had never seen) occurring the day before, I had been obliged to post off to Ireland, and pay proper respect by appearing at the funeral. When I returned the duchess had gone, and Gustave had, half-ironically, consoled my evident annoyance by telling me that he had given such a description of me to his friend that she shared my sorrow, and had left a polite message to that effect. That I was not much consoled needs no saying. That I required consolation will appear not unnatural when I say that the duchess was one of the most brilliant and well-known persons in French society; yes, and outside France also. For she was a cosmopolitan. Her father was French, her mother American; and she had passed two or three years in England before her marriage. She was very pretty, and, report said, as witty as a pretty woman need be. Once she had been rich, but the money was swallowed up by speculation; she and her father (the mother was dead) were threatened with such reduction of means as seemed to them penury; and the marriage with the duke had speedily followed-- the precise degree of unwillingness on the part of Mlle. de Beville being a disputed point. Men said she was forced into the marriage, women very much doubted it; the lady herself gave no indication, and her father declared that the match was one of affection. All this I had heard from common friends; only a series of annoying accidents had prevented the more interesting means of knowledge which acquaintance with the duchess herself would have afforded.

"You have always," said Gustave, "wanted to know her."

I relit my cigar and puffed thoughtfully. It was true that I had rather wished to know her.

"My belief is," he continued, "that though she says 'anybody,' she means you. She knows what friends we are; she knows you are eager to be among her friends; she would guess that I should ask you first."

I despise and hate a man who is not open to flattery: he is a hard, morose, distrustful, cynical being, doubting the honesty of his friends and the worth of his own self. I leant an ear to Gustave's suggestion.

"What she would not guess," he said, throwing his cigarette into the fireplace and rising to his feet, "is that you would refuse when I did ask you. What shall be the reason? Shocked, are you? Or afraid?"

Gustave spoke as though nothing could either shock or frighten him.

"I'm merely considering whether it will amuse me," I returned. "How long are we asked for?"

"That depends on diplomatic events."

"The mission to Algeria?"

"Why, precisely."

I put my hands in my pockets.

"I should certainly be glad, my dear Gustave," said I, "to meet your sister again."

"We take the boat for Cherbourg to-morrow evening!" he cried triumphantly, slapping me on the back. "And, in my sister's name, many thanks! I will make it clear to the duchess why you come."

"No need to make bad blood between them like that," I laughed.

In fine, I was pleased to go; and, on reflection, there was no reason why I should not go. I said as much to Gustave.

"Seeing that everybody is going out of town and the place will be a desert in a week, I'm certainly not wanted here just now."

"And seeing that the duke is gone to Algeria, we certainly are wanted there," said Gustave.

"And a man should go where he is wanted," said I.

"And a man is wanted," said Gustave, "where a lady bids him come."

"It would," I cried, "be impolite not to go."

"It would be dastardly. Besides, think how you will enjoy the memory of it!"

"The memory?" I repeated, pausing in my eager walk up and down.

"It will be a sweet memory," he said.

"Ah!"

"Because, my friend, it is prodigiously unwise--for you."

"And not for you?"

"Why, no. Lady Cynthia--"

He broke off, content to indicate the shield that protected him. But it was too late to draw back.

"Let it be as unwise," said I, "as it will--"

"Or as the duke is," put in Gustave, with a knowing twinkle in his eye.

"Yet it is a plan as delightful--"

"As the duchess is," said Gustave.

And so, for all the excellent reasons which may be collected from the foregoing conversation,--and if carefully tabulated they would, I am persuaded, prove as numerous as weighty,--I went.

CHAPTER II.
The Significance of a Supper-Table.

The Aycons of Aycon Knoll have always been a hard-headed, levelheaded race. We have had no enthusiasms, few ambitions, no illusions, and not many scandals. We keep our heads on our shoulders and our purses in our pockets. We do not rise very high, but we have never sunk. We abide at the Knoll from generation to generation, deeming our continued existence in itself a service to the state and an honor to the house. We think more highly of ourselves than we admit, and allow ourselves to smile when we walk in to dinner behind the new nobility. We grow just a little richer with every decade, and add a field or two to our domains once in five years. The gaps made by falling rents we have filled by judicious purchases of land near rising towns; and we have no doubt that there lies before us a future as long and prosperous as our past has been. We are not universally popular, and we see in the fact a tribute to our valuable qualities.

I venture to mention these family virtues and characteristics because it has been thought in some quarters that I displayed them but to a very slight degree in the course of the expedition on which I was now embarked. The impression is a mistaken one. As I have said before, I did nothing that was not forced upon me. Any of my ancestors would, I am sure, have done the same, had they chanced to be thrown under similar circumstances into the society of Mme. de Saint-Maclou and of the other persons whom I was privileged to meet; and had those other persons happened to act in the manner in which they did when I fell in with them.

Gustave maintained his gayety and good spirits unabated through the trials of our voyage to Cherbourg. The mild mystery that attended our excursion was highly to his taste. He insisted on our coming without servants. He persuaded me to leave no address; obliged to keep himself within touch of the Embassy, he directed letters to be sent to Avranches, where, he explained, he could procure them; for, as he thought it safe to disclose when a dozen miles of sea separated us from the possibility of curious listeners, the house to which we were bound stood about ten miles distant from that town, in a retired and somewhat desolate bit of country lining the seashore.

"My sister says it is the most *triste* place in the world," said he; "but we shall change all that when we arrive."

There was nothing to prevent our arriving very soon to relieve Mlle. de Berensac's depression, for the middle of the next day found us at Avranches, and we spent the afternoon wandering about somewhat aimlessly and staring across the bay at the mass of Mont St. Michel. Directly beneath us as we stood on the hill, and lying in a straight line with the Mount, there was a large square white house, on the very edge of the stretching sand. We were told that it was a convent.

"But the whole place is no livelier than one," said I, yawning. "My dear fellow, why don't we go on?"

"It is right for you to see this interesting town," answered Gustave gravely, but with a merry gleam in his eye. "However, I have ordered a carriage, so be patient."

"For what time?"

"Nine o'clock, when we have dined."

"We are to get there in the dark, then?"

"What reason is there against that?" he asked, smiling.

"None," said I; and I went to pack up my bag.

In my room I chanced to find a *femme-de-chambre*. To her I put a question or two as to the gentry of the neighborhood. She rattled me off a few distinguished names, and ended:

"The duke of Saint-Maclou has also a small château."

"Is he there now?" I asked.

"The duchess only, sir," she answered. "Ah, they tell wonderful stories of her!"

"Do they? Pray, of what kind?"

"Oh, not to her harm, sir; or, at least, not exactly, though to simple country-folk--"

The national shrug was an appropriate ending.

"And the duke?"

"He is a good man," she answered earnestly, "and a very clever man. He is very highly thought of at Paris, sir."

I had hoped, secretly, to hear that he was a villain; but he was a good man. It was a scurvy trick to play on a good man. Well, there was no help for it. I packed my bag with some dawning misgivings; the chambermaid, undisturbed by my presence, went on rubbing the table with some strong-smelling furniture polish.

"At least," she observed, as though there had been no pause, "he gives much to the church and to the poor."

"It may be repentance," said I, looking up with a hopeful air.

"It is possible, sir."

"Or," cried I, with a smile, "hypocrisy?"

The chambermaid's shake of her head refused to accept this idea; but my conscience, fastening on it, found rest. I hesitated no longer. The man was a cunning hypocrite. I would go on cheerfully, secure that he deserved all the bamboozling which the duchess and my friend Gustave might prepare for him.

At nine o'clock, as Gustave had arranged, we started in a heavy carriage drawn by two great white horses and driven by a stolid fat hostler. Slowly we jogged along under the stars, St. Michel being our continual companion on the right hand, as we followed the road round the bay. When we had gone five or six miles, we turned suddenly inland. There were banks on each side of the road now, and we were going uphill; for rising out of the plain there was a sudden low spur of higher ground.

"Is the house at the top?" I asked Gustave.

"Just under the top," said he.

"I shall walk," said I.

The fact is, I had grown intolerably impatient of our slow jog, which had now sunk to a walk.

We jumped out and strode on ahead, soon distancing our carriage, and waking echoes with our merry talk.

"I rather wonder they have not come to meet us," said Gustave. "See, there is the house."

A sudden turn in the road had brought us in sight of it. It was a rather small modern Gothic château. It nestled comfortably below the hill, which rose very steeply immediately behind it. The road along which we were approaching appeared to afford the only access, and no other house was visible. But, desolate as the spot certainly was, the house itself presented a gay appearance, for there were lights in every window from ground to roof.

"She seems to have company," I observed.

"It is that she expects us," answered Gustave. "This illumination is in our honor."

"Come on," said I, quickening my pace; and Gustave burst out laughing.

"I knew you would catch fire when once I got you started!" he cried.

Suddenly a voice struck on my ear--a clear, pleasant voice:

"Was he slow to catch fire, my dear Gustave?"

I started. Gustave looked round.

"It is she," he said. "Where is she?"

"Was he slow to catch fire?" asked the voice again. "Well, he has but just come near the flame"--and a laugh followed the words.

"Slow to light is long to burn," said I, turning to the bank on the left side of the road, for it was thence that the voice came.

A moment later a little figure in white darted down into the road, laughing and panting. She seized Gustave's hand.

"I ran so hard to meet you!" she cried.

"And have you brought Claire with you?" he asked.

"Present your friend to me," commanded the duchess, as though she had not heard his question.

Did I permit myself to guess at such things, I should have guessed the duchess to be about twenty-five years old. She was not tall; her hair was a dark brown, and the color in her cheeks rich but subdued. She moved with extraordinary grace and agility, and seemed never at rest. The one term of praise (if it be one, which I sometimes incline to doubt) that I have never heard applied to her is--dignified.

"It is most charming of you to come, Mr. Aycon," said she. "I've heard so much of you, and you'll be so terribly dull!"

"With yourself, madame, and Mlle. de Berensac--"

"Oh, of course you must say that!" she interrupted. "But come along, supper is ready. How delightful to have supper again! I'm never in good enough spirits to have supper when I'm alone. You'll be terribly uncomfortable, gentlemen. The whole household consists of an old man and five women--counting myself."

"And are they all--?" began Gustave.

"Discreet?" she asked, interrupting again. "Oh, they will not tell the truth! Never fear, my dear Gustave!"

"What news of the duke?" asked he, as we began to walk, the duchess stepping a little ahead of us.

"Oh, the best," said she, with a nod over her shoulder. "None, you know. That's one of your proverbs, Mr. Aycon?"

"Even a proverb is true sometimes," I ventured to remark.

We reached the house and passed through the door, which stood wide open. Crossing the hall, we found ourselves in a small square room, furnished with rose-colored hangings. Here supper was spread. Gustave walked up to the table. The duchess flung herself into an armchair. She had taken her handkerchief out of her pocket, and she held it in front of her lips and seemed to be biting it. Her eyebrows were raised, and her face displayed a comical mixture of amusement and appre-hension. A glance of her eyes at me invited me to share the perilous jest, in which Gustave's demeanor appeared to bear the chief part.

Gustave stood by the table, regarding it with a puzzled air.

"One--two--three!" he exclaimed aloud, counting the covers laid.

The duchess said nothing, but her eyebrows mounted a little higher, till they almost reached her clustering hair.

"One--two--three?" repeated Gustave, in unmistakable questioning. "Does Claire remain upstairs?"

Appeal--amusement--fright--shame--triumph--chased one another across the eyes of Mme. de Saint-Maclou: each made so swift an appearance, so swift an exit, that they seemed to blend in some peculiar personal emotion proper to the duch-ess and to no other woman born. And she bit the handkerchief harder than ever. For the life of me I couldn't help it; I began to laugh; the duchess' face disappeared altogether behind the handkerchief.

"Do you mean to say Claire's not here?" cried Gustave, turning on her swiftly and accusingly.

The head behind the handkerchief was shaken, first timidly, then more emphatically, and a stifled voice vouchsafed the news:

"She left three days ago."

Gustave and I looked at one another. There was a pause. At last I drew a chair back from the table, and said:

"If madame is ready--"

The duchess whisked her handkerchief away and sprang up. She gave one look at Gustave's grave face, and then, bursting into a merry laugh, caught me by the arm, crying:

"Isn't it fun, Mr. Aycon? There's nobody but me! Isn't it fun?"

CHAPTER III.
The Unexpected that Always Happened.

Everything depends on the point of view and is rich in varying aspects. A picture is sublime from one corner of the room, a daub from another; a woman's full face may be perfect, her profile a disappointment; above all, what you admire in yourself becomes highly distasteful in your neighbor. The moral is, I suppose, Tolerance; or if not that, something else which has escaped me.

When the duchess said that "it"--by which she meant the whole position of affairs--was "fun," I laughed; on the other hand, Gustave de Berensac, after one astonished stare, walked to the hall door.

"Where is my carriage?" we heard him ask.

"It has started on the way back three, minutes ago, sir."

"Fetch it back."

"Sir! The driver will gallop down the hill; he could not be overtaken."

"How fortunate!" said I.

"I do not see," observed Mme. de Saint-Maclou, "that it makes all that difference."

She seemed hurt at the serious way in which Gustave took her joke.

"If I had told the truth, you wouldn't have come," she said in justification.

"Not another word is necessary," said I, with a bow.

"Then let us sup," said the duchess, and she took the armchair at the head of the table.

We began to eat and drink, serving ourselves. Presently Gustave entered, stood regarding us for a moment, and then flung himself into the third chair and poured out a glass of wine. The duchess took no notice of him.

"Mlle, de Berensac was called away?" I suggested.

"She was called away," answered the duchess.

"Suddenly?"

"No," said the duchess, her eyes again full of complicated expressions. I laughed. Then she broke out in a plaintive cry: "Oh! were you ever dying--dying--dying of weariness?"

Gustave made no reply; the frown on his face persisted.

"Isn't it a pity," I asked, "to wreck a pleasant party for the sake of a fine distinction? The presence of Mlle. de Berensac would have infinitely increased our pleasure; but how would it have diminished our crime?"

"I wish I had known you sooner, Mr. Aycon," said the duchess; "then I needn't have asked him at all."

I bowed, but I was content with things as they were. The duchess sat with the air of a child who has been told that she is naughty, but declines to accept the statement. I was puzzled at the stern morality exhibited by my friend Gustave. His next remark threw some light on his feelings.

"Heavens! if it became known, what would be thought?" he demanded suddenly.

"If one thinks of what is thought," said the duchess with a shrug, "one is--"

"A fool," said I, "or--a lover!"

"Ah!" cried the duchess, a smile coming on her lips. "If it is that, I'll forgive you, my dear Gustave. Whose good opinion do you fear to lose?"

"I write," said Gustave, with a rhetorical gesture, "to say that I am going to the house of some friends to meet my sister!"

"Oh, you write?" we murmured.

"My sister writes to say she is not there!"

"Oh, she writes?" we murmured again.

"And it is thought--"

"By whom?" asked the duchess.

"By Lady Cynthia Chillingdon," said I.

"That it is a trick--a device--a deceit!" continued poor Gustave.

"It was decidedly indiscreet of you to come," said the duchess reprovingly. "How was I to know about Lady Cynthia? If I had known about Lady Cynthia, I would not have asked you; I would have asked Mr. Aycon only. Or perhaps you also, Mr. Aycon--"

"Madame," said I, "I am alone in the world."

"Where has Claire gone to?" asked Gustave.

"Paris," pouted the duchess.

Gustave rose, flinging his napkin on the table.

"I shall follow her to-morrow," he said. "I suppose you'll go back to England, Gilbert?"

If Gustave left us, it was my unhesitating resolve to return to England.

"I suppose I shall," said I.

"I suppose you must," said the duchess ruefully. "Oh, isn't it exasperating? I had planned it all so delightfully!"

"If you had told the truth--" began Gustave.

"I should not have had a preacher to supper," said the duchess sharply; then she fell to laughing again.

"Is Mlle. de Berensac irrecoverable?" I suggested.

"Why, yes. She has gone to take her turn of attendance on your rich old aunt, Gustave."

I think that there was a little malice in the duchess' way of saying this.

There seemed nothing more to be done. The duchess herself did not propose to defy conventionality to the extent of inviting me to stay. To do her justice, as soon as the inevitable was put before her, she accepted it with good grace, and, after supper, busied herself in discovering the time and manner in which her guests might pursue their respective journeys. I may be flattering myself, but I thought that she displayed a melancholy satisfaction on discovering that Gustave de Berensac must leave at ten o'clock the next morning, whereas I should be left to kick my heels in idleness at Cherbourg if I set out before five in the afternoon.

"Oh, you can spend the time *en route*," said Gustave. "It will be better."

The duchess looked at me; I looked at the duchess.

"My dear Gustave," said I, "you are very considerate. You could not do more if I also were in love with Lady Cynthia."

"Nor," said the duchess, "if I were quite unfit to be spoken to."

"If my remaining till the afternoon will not weary the duchess--" said I.

"The duchess will endure it," said she, with a nod and a smile.

Thus it was settled, a shake of the head conveying Gustave's judgment. And soon after, Mme. de Saint-Maclou bade us good-night. Tired with my journey, and (to tell the truth) a little out of humor with my friend, I was not long in seeking my bed. At the top of the stairs a group of three girls were gossiping; one of them handed me a candle and flung open the door of my room with a roguish smile on her broad good-tempered face.

"One of the greatest virtues of women," said I pausing on the threshold, "is fidelity."

"We are devoted to Mme. la Duchesse," said the girl.

"Another, hardly behind it, is discretion," I continued.

"Madame inculcates it on us daily," said she. I took out a napoleon.

"Ladies," said I, placing the napoleon in the girl's hand, "I am obliged for your kind attentions. Good-night!" and I shut the door on the sound of a pleased, excited giggling. I love to hear such sounds; they make me laugh myself, for joy that this old world, in spite of everything, holds so much merriment; and to their jovial lullaby I fell asleep,

Moreover--the duchess teaching discretion! There can have been nothing like it since Baby Charles and Steenie conversed within the hearing of King James! But, then discretion has two meanings--whereof the one is "Do it not," and the other "Tell it not." Considering of this ambiguity, I acquitted the duchess of hypocrisy.

At ten o'clock the next morning we got rid of my dear friend Gustave de Berensac. Candor compels me to put the statement in that form; for the gravity which had fallen upon him the night before endured till the morning, and he did not flinch from administering something very like a lecture to his hostess. His last words were an invitation to me to get into the carriage and start with him. When I suavely declined, he told me that I should regret it. It comforts me to think that his prophecy, though more than once within an ace of the most ample fulfillment, yet in the end was set at naught by the events which followed.

Gustave rolled down the hill, the duchess sighed relief.

"Now," said she, "we can enjoy ourselves fora few hours, Mr. Aycon. And after that--solitude!"

I was really very sorry for the duchess. Evidently society and gayety were necessary as food and air to her, and her churl of a husband denied them. My opportunity was short, but I laid myself out to make the most of it. I could give her nothing more than a pleasant memory, but I determined to do that.

We spent the greater part of the day in a ramble through the woods that lined the slopes of the hill behind the house; and all through the hours the duchess chatted about herself, her life, her family--and then about the duke. If the hints she gave were to be trusted, her husband deserved little consideration at her hands, and, at the worst, the plea of reprisal might offer some excuse for her, if she had need of one. But she denied the need, and here I was inclined to credit her. For with me, as with Gustave de Berensac before the shadow of Lady Cynthia came between, she was, most distinctly, a "good comrade." Sentiment made no appearance in our conversation, and, as the day ruthlessly wore on, I regretted honestly that I must go in deference to a conventionality which seemed, in this case at least--Heaven forbid that I should indulge in general theories--to mask no reality. Yet she was delightful by virtue of the vitality in her; and the woods echoed again and again with our laughter.

At four o'clock we returned sadly to the house, where the merry girls busied themselves in preparing a repast for me. The duchess insisted on sharing my meal.

"I shall go supperless to bed to-night," said she; and we sat down glum as two children going back to school.

Suddenly there was a commotion outside; the girls were talking to one another in rapid eager tones. The duchess raised her head, listening. Then she turned to me, asking:

"Can you hear what they say?"

"I can distinguish nothing except 'Quick, quick!'"

As I spoke the door was thrown open, and two rushed in, the foremost saying: "Again, madame, again!"

"Impossible!" exclaimed the duchess, starting up.

"No, it is true. Jean was out, snaring a rabbit, and caught sight of the carriage."

"What carriage? Whose carriage?" I asked.

"Why, my husband's," said the duchess, quite calmly. "It is a favorite trick of his to surprise us. But Algeria! We thought we were safe with Algeria. He must travel underground like a mole, Suzanne, or we should have heard."

"Oh, one hears nothing here!"

"And what," said the duchess, "are we to do with Mr. Aycon?"

"I can solve that," I observed. "I'm off."

"But he'll see you!" cried the girl. "He is but a half-mile off."

"Mr. Aycon could take the side-path," said the duchess.

"The duke would see him before he reached it," said the girl. "He would be in sight for nearly fifty yards."

"Couldn't I hide in the bushes?" I asked.

"I hate anything that looks suspicious," remarked the duchess, still quite calm; "and if he happened to see you, it would look rather suspicious! And he has got eyes like a cat's for anything of that sort."

There was no denying that it would look suspicious if I were caught hiding in the bushes. I sat silent, having no other suggestion to make.

Suzanne, with a readiness not born, I hope, of practice, came to the rescue with a clever suggestion.

"The English groom whom madame dismissed a week ago--" said she. "Why should not the gentleman pass as the groom? The man would not take his old clothes away, for he had bought new ones, and they are still here. The gentleman would put them on and walk past--voilà."

"Can you look like a groom?" asked the duchess. "If he speaks to you, make your French just a *little* worse"--and she smiled.

They were all so calm and businesslike that it would have seemed disobliging and absurd to make difficulties.

"We can send your luggage soon, you know," said the duchess. "You had better hide Mr. Aycon's luggage in your room, Suzanne. Really, I am afraid you ought to be getting ready, Mr. Aycon."

The point of view again! By virtue of the duchess' calmness and Suzanne's cool readiness, the proceeding seemed a most ordinary one. Five minutes later I presented myself to the duchess, dressed in a villainous suit of clothes, rather too tight for me, and wearing a bad hat rakishly cocked over one eye. The duchess surveyed me with great curiosity.

"Fortunately the duke is not a very clever man," said she. "Oh, by the way, your name's George Sampson, and you come from Newmarket; and you are leaving because you took more to drink than was good for you. Good-by, Mr. Aycon. I do hope that we shall meet again under pleasanter circumstances."

"They could not be pleasanter--but they might be more prolonged," said I.

"It was so good of you to come," she said, pressing my hand.

"The carriage is but a quarter of a mile off!" cried Suzanne warningly.

"How very annoying it is! I wish to Heaven the Algerians had eaten the duke!"

"I shall not forget my day here," I assured her.

"You won't? It's charming of you. Oh, how dull it will be now! It only wanted the arrival of--Well, good-by!"

And with a final and long pressure of the duchess' hand, I, in the garb and personality of George Sampson, dismissed for drunkenness, walked out of the gate of the château.

"One thing," I observed to myself as I started, "would seem highly probable--and that is, that this sort of thing has happened before."

The idea did not please me. I like to do things first.

CHAPTER IV.
The Duchess Defines Her Position.

I walked on at a leisurely pace; the heavy carriage was very near the top of the hill. In about three minutes' time we met. There sat alone in the carriage a tall dark man, with a puffy white face, a heavy mustache, and stern cold eyes. He was smoking a cigar. I plucked my hat from my head and made as if to pass by.

"Who's this?" he called out, stopping the carriage.

I began to recite my lesson in stumbling French.

"Why, what are you? Oh, you're English! Then in Heaven's name, speak English--not that gabble." And then he repeated his order, "Speak English," in English, and continued in that language, which he spoke with stiff formal correctness.

He heard my account of myself with unmoved face.

"Have you any writings--any testimonials?" he asked.

"No, my lord," I stammered, addressing him in style I thought most natural to my assumed character.

"That's a little curious, isn't it? You become intoxicated everywhere, perhaps?"

"I've never been intoxicated in my life, my lord," said I, humbly but firmly.

"Then you dispute the justice of your dismissal?"

"Yes, my lord." I thought such protest due to my original.

He looked at me closely, smoking his cigar the while.

"You made love to the chambermaids?" he asked suddenly.

"No, my lord. One evening, my lord, it was very hot, and--and the wine, my lord--"

"Then you were intoxicated?"

I fumbled with my hat, praying that the fellow would move on.

"What servants are there?" he asked, pointing to the house.

"Four maids, my lord, and old Jean."

Again he meditated; then he said sharply:

"Have you ever waited at table?"

We have all, I suppose, waited at table--in one sense. Perhaps that may save my remark from untruth.

"Now and then, my lord," I answered, wondering what he would be at.

"I have guests arriving to-morrow," he said. "My man comes with them, but the work will perhaps be too much for him. Are you willing to stay and help? I will pay you the same wages."

I could have laughed in his face; but duty seemed to point to seriousness.

"I'm very sorry, my lord--" I began.

"What, have you got another place?"

"No, my lord; not exactly."

"Then get up on the front seat. Or do you want your employers to say you are disobliging as well as drunken?"

"But the lady sent me--"

"You may leave that to me. Come, jump up! Don't keep me waiting!"

Doubtfully I stood in the road, the duke glaring at me with impatient anger. Then he leaned forward and said:

"You are curiously reluctant, sir, to earn your living. I don't understand it. I must make some inquiries about you."

I detected suspicion dawning in his eyes. He was a great man; I did not know what hindrances he might not be able to put in the way of my disappearance. And what would happen if he made his inquiries? Inquiries might mean searching, and I carried a passport in the name of Gilbert Aycon.

Such share had prudence; the rest must be put down to the sudden impulse of amusement which seized me. It was but for a day or two! Then I could steal away. Meanwhile what would not the face of the duchess say, when I rode up on the front seat!

"I--I was afraid I should not give satisfaction," I muttered.

"You probably won't," said he. "I take you from necessity, not choice, my friend. Up with you!"

And I got up beside the driver--not, luckily, the one who had brought Gustave de Berensac and myself the day before--and the carriage resumed its slow climb up the hill.

We stopped at the door. I jumped down and assisted my new master.

The door was shut. Nobody was to be seen; evidently we were not expected. The duke smiled sardonically, opened the door and walked in, I just behind. Suzanne was sweeping the floor. With one glance at the duke and myself, she sprang back, with a cry of most genuine surprise.

"Oh, you're mighty surprised, aren't you?" sneered the duke. "Old Jean didn't scuttle away to tell you then? You keep a good watch, young woman. Your mistress' orders, eh?"

Still Suzanne stared--and at me. The duke chuckled.

"Yes, he's back again," said he, "so you must make the best of it, my girl. Where's the duchess?"

"In--in--in her sitting-room, M. le Duc."

"'In--in--in,'" he echoed mockingly. Then he stepped swiftly across the hall and flung the door suddenly open. I believe he thought that he really had surprised Jean's slow aged scamper ahead of him.

"Silence for your life!" I had time to whisper to Suzanne; and then I followed him. There might be more "fun" to come.

The duchess was sitting with a book in her hand. I was half-hidden by the duke, and she did not see me. She looked up, smiled, yawned, and held out her hand.

"I hardly expected you, Armand," said she. "I thought you were in Algeria."

Anybody would have been annoyed; there is no doubt that the Duke of Saint-Maclou was very much annoyed.

"You don't seem overjoyed at the surprise," said he gruffly.

"You are always surprising me," she answered, lifting her eyebrows.

Suddenly he turned round, saying "Sampson!" and then turned to her, adding:

"Here's another old friend for you." And he seized me by the shoulder and pulled me into the room.

The duchess sprang to her feet, crying out in startled tones, "Back?"

I kept my eyes glued to the floor, wondering what would happen next, thinking that it would be, likely enough, a personal conflict with my master.

"Yes, back," said he. "I am sorry, madame, if it is not your pleasure, for it chances to be mine."

His sneer gave the duchess a moment's time. I felt her regarding me, and I looked up cautiously. The duke still stood half a pace in front of me, and the message of my glance sped past him unperceived.

Then came what I had looked for--the gradual dawning of the position on the duchess, and the reflection of that dawning light in those wonderful eyes of hers. She clasped her hands, and drew in her breath in a long "Oh!" It spoke utter amusement and delight. What would the duke make of it? He did not know what to make of it, and glared at her in angry bewilderment. Her quick wit saw the blunder she had been betrayed into. She said "Oh!" again, but this time it expressed nothing except a sense of insult and indignation.

"What's that man here for?" she asked.

"Because I have engaged him to assist my household."

"I had dismissed him," she said haughtily.

"I must beg you to postpone the execution of your decree," said he. "I have need of a servant, and I have no time to find another."

"What need is there of another? Is not Lafleur here?" (She was playing her part well now.)

"Lafleur comes to-morrow; but he will not be enough."

"Not enough--for you and me?"

"Our party will be larger to-morrow."

"More surprises?" she asked, sinking back into her chair.

"If it be a surprise that I should invite my friends to my house," he retorted.

"And that you should not consult your wife," she said, with a smile.

He turned to me, bethinking himself, I suppose, that the conversation was not best suited for the ears of the groom.

"Go and join your fellow-servants; and see that you behave yourself this time."

I bowed and was about to withdraw, when the duchess motioned me to stop. For an instant her eyes rested on mine. Then she said, in gentle tones:

"I am glad, Sampson, that the duke thinks it safe to give you an opportunity of retrieving your character."

"That for his character!" said the duke, snapping his fingers. "I want him to help when Mme. and Mlle. Delhasse are here."

On the words the duchess went red in the face, and then white, and sprang up, declaring aloud in resolute, angry tones, that witnessed the depth of her feelings in the matter: "I will not receive Mlle. Delhasse!"

I was glad I had not missed that: it was a new aspect of my little friend the duchess. Alas, my pleasure was short-lived! for the duke, his face full of passion, pointed to the door, saying "Go!" and, cursing his regard for the dignity of the family, I went.

In the hall I paused. At first I saw nobody. Presently a rosy, beaming face peered at me over the baluster halfway up the stairs, and Suzanne stole cautiously down, her finger on her lips.

"But what does it mean, sir?" she whispered.

"It means," said I, "that the duke takes me for the dismissed groom--and has re-engaged me."

"And you've come?" she cried softly, clasping her hands in amazement.

"Doesn't it appear so?"

"And you're going to stay, sir?"

"Ah, that's another matter. But--for the moment, yes."

"As a servant?"

"Why not--in such good company?"

"Does madame know?"

"Yes, she knows, Suzanne. Come, show me the way to my quarters; and no more 'sir' just now."

We were standing by the stairs. I looked up and saw the other girls clustered on the landing above us.

"Go and tell them," I said. "Warn them to show no surprise. Then come back and show me the way."

Suzanne, her mirth half-startled out of her but yet asserting its existence in dimples round her mouth, went on her errand. I leaned against the lowest baluster and waited.

Suddenly the door of the duchess' room was flung open and she came out. She stood for an instant on the threshold. She turned toward the interior of the room and she stamped her foot on the parqueted floor.

"No--no--no!" she said passionately, and flung the door close behind her, to the accompaniment of a harsh, scornful laugh.

Involuntarily I sprang forward to meet her. But she was better on her guard than I.

"Not now," she whispered, "but I must see you soon--this evening--after dinner. Suzanne will arrange it. You must help me, Mr. Aycon; I'm in trouble."

"With all my power!" I whispered, and with a glance of thanks she sped upstairs. I saw her stop and speak to the group of girls, talking to them in an eager whisper. Then, followed by two of them, she pursued her way upstairs.

Suzanne came down and approached me, saying simply, "Come," and led the way toward the servants' quarters. I followed her, smiling; I was about to make acquaintance with a new side of life.

Yet at the same time I was wondering who Mlle. Delhasse might chance to be: the name seemed familiar to me, and yet for the moment I could not trace it. And then I slapped my thigh in the impulse of my discovery.

"By Jove, Marie Delhasse the singer!" cried I, in English.

"Sir, sir, for Heaven's sake be quiet!" whispered Suzanne.

"You are perfectly right," said I, with a nod of approbation.

"And this is the pantry," said Suzanne, for all the world as though nothing had happened. "And in that cupboard you will find Sampson's livery."

"Is it a pretty one?" I asked.

"You, sir, will look well in it," said she, with that delicate evasive flattery that I love. "Would not you, sir, look well in anything?" she meant.

And while I changed my traveling suit for the livery, I remembered more about Marie Delhasse, and, among other things, that the Duke of Saint-Maclou was rumored to be her most persistent admirer. Some said that she favored him; others denied it with more or less conviction and indignation. But, whatever might chance to be the truth about that, it was plain that the duchess had something to say for herself when she declined to receive the lady. Her refusal was no idle freak, but a fixed determination, to which she would probably adhere. And, in fact, adhere to it she did, even under some considerable changes of circumstance.

CHAPTER V.
A Strategic Retreat.

The arrival of the duke, aided perhaps by his bearing toward his wife and toward me, had a somewhat curious effect on me. I will not say that I felt at liberty to fall in love with the duchess; but I felt the chain of honor, which had hitherto bound me from taking any advantage of her indiscretion, growing weaker; and I also perceived the possibility of my inclinations beginning to strain on the weakened chain. On this account, among others, I resolved, as I sat in the pantry drinking a glass of wine with which Suzanne kindly provided me, that my sojourn in the duke's household should be of the shortest. Moreover, I was not amused; I was not a real groom; the maids treated me with greater distance and deference than before; I lost the entertainment of upstairs, and did not gain the interest of downstairs. The absurd position must be ended. I would hear what the duchess wanted of me; then I would go, leaving Lafleur to grapple with his increased labors as best he could. True, I should miss Marie Delhasse. Well, young men are foolish.

"Perhaps," said I to myself with a sigh, "it's just as well."

I did not wait at table that night; the duchess was shut up in her own apartment: the duke took nothing but an omelette and a cup of coffee; these finished, he summoned Suzanne and her assistants to attend him on the bedroom floor, and I heard him giving directions for the lodging of the expected guests. Apparently they were to be received, although the duchess would not receive them. Not knowing what to make of that situation, I walked out into the garden and lit my pipe; I had clung to that in spite of my change of raiment.

Presently Suzanne looked out. A call from the duke proclaimed that she had stolen a moment. She nodded, pointed to the narrow gravel path which led into the shrubbery, and hastily withdrew. I understood, and strolled carelessly along the path till I reached the shrubbery. There another little path, running nearly at right angles to that by which I had come, opened before me. I strolled some little way along, and finding myself entirely hidden from the house by the intervening trees, I sat down on a rude wooden bench to wait patiently till I should be wanted. For the duchess I should have had to wait some time, but for company I did not wait long; after about ten minutes I perceived a small, spare, dark-complexioned man coming along the path toward me and toward the house. He must have made a short cut from the road, escaping the winding of the carriage-way. He wore decent but rather shabby clothes, and carried a small valise in his hand. Stopping opposite to me, he raised his hat and seemed to scan my neat blue brass-buttoned coat and white cords with interest.

"You belong to the household of the duke, sir?" he asked, with a polite lift of his hat.

I explained that I did--for the moment.

"Then you think of leaving, sir?"

"I do," I said, "as soon as I can; I am only engaged for the time."

"You do not happen to know, sir, if the duke requires a well-qualified indoor servant? I should be most grateful if you would present me to him. I heard in Paris that a servant had left him; but he started so suddenly that I could not get access to him, and I have followed him here."

"It's exactly what he does want, I believe, sir," said I. "If I were you, I would go to the house and obtain entrance. The duke expects guests to-morrow."

"But yourself, sir? Are not your services sufficient for the present?"

"As you perceive," said I, indicating my attire, "I am not an indoor servant. I am but a makeshift in that capacity."

He smiled a polite remonstrance at my modesty, adding:

"You think, then, I might have a chance?"

"An excellent one, I believe. Turn to the left, there by the chestnut tree, and you will find yourself within a minute's walk of the front door."

He bowed, raised his hat, and trotted off, moving with a quick, shuffling, short-stepping gait. I lit another pipe and yawned. I hoped the duke would engage this newcomer and let me go about my business; and I fancied that he would, for the fellow looked dapper, sharp, and handy. And the duchess? I was so disturbed to find myself disturbed at the thought of the duchess that I exclaimed:

"By Jove, I'd better go! By Jove, I had!"

A wishing-cap, or rather a hoping-cap--for if a man who is no philosopher may have an opinion, we do not always wish and hope for the same thing--could have done no more for me than the chance of Fate; for at the moment the duke's voice called "Sampson!" loudly from the house. I ran in obedience to his summons. He stood in the porch with the little stranger by him; and the stranger wore a deferential, but extremely well-satisfied smile.

"Here, you," said the duke to me, "you can make yourself scarce as soon as you like. I've got a better servant, aye, and a sober one. There's ten francs for you. Now be off!"

I felt it incumbent on me to appear a little aggrieved:

"Am I to go to-night?" I asked. "Where can I get to to-night, my lord?"

"What's that to me? I dare say if you stand old Jean a franc, he'll give you a lift to the nearest inn. Tell him he may take a farm-horse."

Really the duke was treating me with quite as much civility as I have seen many of my friends extend to their servants. I had nothing to complain of. I bowed, and was about to turn away, when the duchess appeared in the porch.

"What is it, Armand?" she asked. "You are sending Sampson away after all?"

"I could not deny your request," said he in mockery. "Moreover, I have found a better servant."

The stranger almost swept the ground in obeisance before the lady of the house.

"You are very changeable," said the duchess.

I saw vexation in her face.

"My dearest, your sex cannot have a monopoly of change. I change a bad servant--as you yourself think him--for a good one. Is that remarkable?"

The duchess said not another word, but turned into the house and disappeared. The duke followed her. The stranger, with a bow to me, followed him. I was left alone.

"Certainly I am not wanted," said I to myself; and, having arrived at this conclusion, I sought out old Jean. The old fellow was only too ready to drive me to

Avranches or anywhere else for five francs, and was soon busy putting his horse in the shafts. I sought out Suzanne, got her to smuggle my luggage downstairs, gave her a parting present, took off my livery and put on the groom's old suit, and was ready to leave the house of M. de Saint-Maclou.

At nine o'clock my short servitude ended. As soon as a bend in the road hid us from the house I opened my portmanteau, got out my own clothes, and, sub æthere, changed my raiment, putting on a quiet suit of blue, and presenting George Sampson's rather obtrusive garments (which I took the liberty of regarding as a perquisite) to Jean, who received them gladly. I felt at once a different being--so true it is that the tailor makes the man.

"You are well out of that," grunted old Jean. "If he'd discovered you, he'd have had you out and shot you!"

"He is a good shot?"

"Mon Dieu!" said Jean with an expressiveness which was a little disquieting; for it was on the cards that the duke might still find me out. And I was not a practiced shot--not at my fellow-men, I mean. Suddenly I leaped up.

"Good Heavens!" I cried. "I forgot! The duchess wanted me. Stop, stop!"

With a jerk Jean pulled up his horse, and gazed at me.

"You can't go back like that," he said, with a grin. "You'll have to put on these clothes again," and he pointed to the discarded suit.

"I very nearly forgot the duchess," said I. To tell the truth, I was at first rather proud of my forgetfulness; it argued a complete triumph over that unruly impulse at which I have hinted. But it also smote me with remorse. I leaped to the ground.

"You must wait while I run back."

"He will shoot you after all," grinned Jean.

"The devil take him!" said I, picturing the poor duchess utterly forsaken--at the mercy of Delhasses, husband, and what not.

I declare, as my deliberate opinion, that there is nothing more dangerous than for a man almost to forget a lady who has shown him favor. If he can quite forget her--and will be so unromantic--why, let him, and perhaps small harm done. But almost--That leaves him at the mercy of every generous self-reproach. He is ready to do anything to prove that she was every second in his memory.

I began to retrace my steps toward the château.

"I shall get the sack over this!" called Jean.

"You shall come to no harm by that, if you do," I assured him.

But hardly had I--my virtuous pride now completely smothered by my tender remorse--started on my ill-considered return journey, when, just as had happened to Gustave de Berensac and myself the evening before, a slim figure ran down from the bank by the roadside. It was the duchess. The short cut had served her. She was hardly out of breath this time; and she appeared composed and in good spirits.

"I thought for a moment you'd forgotten me, but I knew you wouldn't do that, Mr. Aycon."

Could I resist such trust?

"Forget you, madame?" I cried. "I would as soon forget--"

"So I knew you'd wait for me."

"Here I am, waiting faithfully," said I.

"That's right," said the duchess. "Take this, please, Mr. Aycon."

"This" was a small handbag. She gave it to me, and began to walk toward the cart, where Jean was placidly smoking a long black cheroot.

"You wished to speak to me?" I suggested, as I walked by her.

"I can do it," said the duchess, reaching the cart, "as we go along."

Even Jean took his cheroot from his lips. I jumped back two paces.

"I beg your pardon!" I exclaimed, "As we go along, did you say?"

"It will be better," said the duchess, getting into the cart (unassisted by me, I am sorry to say). "Because he may find out I'm gone, and come after us, you know."

Nothing seemed more likely; I was bound to admit that.

"Get in, Mr. Aycon," continued the duchess. And then she suddenly began to talk English. "I told him I shouldn't stay in the house if Mlle. Delhasse came. He didn't believe me; well, he'll see now. I couldn't stay, could I? Why don't you get in?"

Half dazed, I got in. I offered no opinion on the question of Mlle. Delhasse: to begin with, I knew very little about it; in the second place there seemed to me to be a more pressing question.

"Quick, Jean!" said the duchess.

And we lumbered on at a trot, Jean twisting his cheroot round and round, and grunting now and again. The old man's face said, plain as words.

"Yes, I shall get the sack; and you'll be shot!"

I found my tongue.

"Was this what you wanted me for?" I asked.

"Of course," said the duchess, speaking French again.

"But you can't come with me!" I cried in unfeigned horror.

The duchess looked up; she fixed her eyes on me for a moment; her eyes grew round, her brows lifted. Then her lips curved: she blushed very red; and she burst into the merriest fit of laughter.

"Oh, dear!" laughed the duchess. "Oh, what fun, Mr. Aycon!"

"It seems to me rather a serious matter," I ventured to observe. "Leaving out all question of--of what's correct, you know" (I became very apologetic at this point), "it's just a little risky, isn't it?"

Jean evidently thought so; he nodded solemnly over his cheroot.

The duchess still laughed; indeed, she was wiping her eyes with her handkerchief.

"What an opinion to have of me!" she gasped at last. "I'm not coming with you, Mr. Aycon."

I dare say my face showed relief: I don't know that I need be ashamed of that. My change of expression, however, set the duchess a-laughing again.

"I never saw a man look so glad," said she gayly. Yet somewhere, lurking in the recesses of her tone--or was it of her eyes?--there was a little reproach, a little challenge. And suddenly I felt less glad: a change of feeling which I do not seek to defend.

"Then where are you going?" I asked in much curiosity.

"I am going," said the duchess, assuming in a moment a most serious air, "into religious retirement for a few days."

"Religious retirement?" I echoed in surprise.

"Are you thinking it's not my métier?" she asked, her eyes gleaming again.

"But where?" I cried.

"Why, there, to be sure." And she pointed to where the square white convent stood on the edge of the bay, under the hill of Avranches. "There, at the convent. The Mother Superior is my friend, and will protect me."

The duchess spoke as though the guillotine were being prepared for her. I sat silent. The situation was becoming rather too complicated for my understanding. Unfortunately, however, it was to become more complicated still; for the duchess, turning to the English tongue again, laid a hand on my arm and said in her most coaxing tones:

"And you, my dear Mr. Aycon, are going to stay a few days in Avranches."

"Not an hour!" would have expressed the resolve of my intellect. But we are not all intellect; and what I actually said was:

"What for?"

"In case," said the duchess, "I want you, Mr. Aycon."

"I will stay," said I, nodding, "just a few days at Avranches."

We were within half a mile of that town. The convent gleamed white in the moonlight about three hundred yards to the left. The duchess took her little bag, jumped lightly down, kissed her hand to me, and walked off.

Jean had made no comment at all--the duchess' household was hard to surprise. I could make none. And we drove in silence into Avranches.

When there before with Gustave, I had put up at a small inn at the foot of the hill. Now I drove up to the summit and stopped before the principal hotel. A waiter ran out, cast a curious glance at my conveyance, and lifted my luggage down.

"Let me know if you get into any trouble for being late," said I to Jean, giving him another five francs.

He nodded and drove off, still chewing the stump of his cheroot.

"Can I have a room?" I asked, turning to the waiter.

"Certainly, sir," said he, catching up my bag in his hand.

"I am just come," said I, "from Mont St. Michel."

A curious expression spread over the waiter's face. I fancy he knew old Jean and the cart by sight; but he spread out his hands and smiled.

"Monsieur," said he with the incomparable courtesy of the French nation, "has come from wherever monsieur pleases."

"That," said I, giving him a trifle, "is an excellent understanding."

Then I walked into the salle-à-manger, and almost into the arms of an extraordinarily handsome girl who was standing just inside the door.

"This is really an eventful day," I thought to myself.

CHAPTER VI.
A Hint of Something Serious.

Occurrences such as this induce in a man of imagination a sense of sudden shy intimacy. The physical encounter seems to typify and foreshadow some intermingling of destiny. This occurs with peculiar force when the lady is as beautiful as was the girl I saw before me.

"I beg your pardon, madame," said I, with a whirl of my hat.

"I beg your pardon, sir," said the lady, with an inclination of her head.

"One is so careless in entering rooms hurriedly," I observed.

"Oh, but it is stupid to stand just by the door!" insisted the lady.

Conscious that she was scanning my appearance, I could but return the compliment. She was very tall, almost as tall as I was myself; you would choose to call her stately, rather than slender. She was very fair, with large lazy blue eyes and a lazy smile to match. In all respects she was the greatest contrast to the Duchess of Saint-Maclou.

"You were about to pass out?" said I, holding the door.

She bowed; but at the moment another lady--elderly, rather stout, and, to speak it plainly, of homely and unattractive aspect--whom I had not hitherto perceived, called from a table at the other end of the room where she was sitting:

"We ought to start early to-morrow."

The younger lady turned her head slowly toward the speaker.

"My dear mother," said she, "I never start early. Besides, this town is interesting--the landlord says so."

"But he wishes us to arrive for déjeuner."

"We will take it here. Perhaps we will drive over in the afternoon--perhaps the next day."

And the young lady gazed at her mother with an air of indifference--or rather it seemed to me strangely like one of aversion and defiance.

"My dear!" cried the elder in consternation. "My dearest Marie!"

"It is just as I thought," said I to myself complacently.

Marie Delhasse--for beyond doubt it was she--walked slowly across the room and sat down by her mother. I took a table nearer the door; the waiter appeared, and I ordered a light supper. Marie poured out a glass of wine from a bottle on the table; apparently they had been supping. They began to converse together in low tones. My repast arriving, I fell to. A few moments later, I heard Marie say, in her composed indolent tones:

"I'm not sure I shall go at all. ***Entre nous***, he bores me."

I stole a glance at Mme. Delhasse. Consternation was writ large on her face, and suspicion besides. She gave her daughter a quick sidelong glance, and a frown gathered on her brow. So far as I heard, however, she attempted no remonstrance. She rose, wrapping a shawl round her, and made for the door. I sprang up and opened it; she walked out. Marie drew a chair to the fire and sat down with her back to me, toasting her feet--for the summer night had turned chilly. I finished my supper. The clock struck half-past eleven. I stifled a yawn; one smoke and then to the bed was my programme.

Marie Delhasse turned her head half-round.

"You must not," said she, "let me prevent you having your cigarette. I should set you at ease by going to bed, but I can't sleep so early, and upstairs the fire is not lighted."

I thanked her and approached the fire. She was gazing into it meditatively. Presently she looked up.

"Smoke, sir," she said imperiously but languidly.

I obeyed her, and stood looking down at her, admiring her stately beauty.

"You have passed the day here?" she asked, gazing again into the fire.

"In this neighborhood," said I, with discreet vagueness.

"You have been able to pass the time?"

"Oh, certainly!" That had not been my difficulty.

"There is, of course," she said wearily, "Mont St. Michel. But can you imagine anyone living in such a country?"

"Unless Fate set one here--" I began.

"I suppose that's it," she interrupted.

"You are going to make a stay here?"

"I am," she answered slowly, "on my way to--I don't know where."

I was scrutinizing her closely now, for her manner seemed to witness more than indolence; irresolution, vacillation, discomfort, asserted their presence. I could not make her out, but her languid indifference appeared more assumed than real.

With another upward glance, she said:

"My name is Marie Delhasse."

"It is a well-known name," said I with a bow.

"You have heard of me?"

"Yes."

"What?" she asked quickly, wheeling half-round and facing me.

"That you are a great singer," I answered simply.

"Ah, I'm not all voice! What about me? A woman is more than an organ pipe. What about me?"

Her excitement contrasted with the langour she had displayed before.

"Nothing," said I, wondering that she should ask a stranger such a question. She glanced at me for an instant. I threw my eyes up to the ceiling.

"It is false!" she said quietly; but the trembling of her hands belied her composure.

The tawdry gilt clock on the mantelpiece by me ticked through a long silence. The last act of the day's comedy seemed set for a more serious scene.

"Why do you ask a stranger a question like that?" I said at last, giving utterance to the thought that puzzled me.

"Whom should I ask? And I like your face--no, not because it is handsome. You are English, sir?"

"Yes, I am English. My name is Gilbert Aycon."

"Aycon--Aycon! It is a little difficult to say it as you say it."

Her thoughts claimed her again. I threw my cigarette into the fire, and stood waiting her pleasure. But she seemed to have no more to say, for she rose from the seat and held out her hand to me.

"Will you 'shake hands?'" she said, the last two words in English; and she smiled again.

I hastened to do as she asked me, and she moved toward the door.

"Perhaps," she said, "I shall see you to-morrow morning."

"I shall be here." Then I added: "I could not help hearing you talk of moving elsewhere."

She stood still in the middle of the room; she opened her lips to speak, shut them again, and ended by saying nothing more than:

"Yes, we talked of it. My mother wishes it. Good-night, Mr. Aycon."

I bade her good-night, and she passed slowly through the door, which I closed behind her. I turned again to the fire, saying:

"What would the duchess think of that?"

I did not even know what I thought of it myself; of one thing only I felt sure---that what I had heard of Marie Delhasse was not all that there was to learn about her.

I was lodged in a large room on the third floor, and when I awoke the bright sun beamed on the convent where, as I presume, Mme. de Saint-Maclou lay, and on the great Mount beyond it in the distance. I have never risen with a more lively sense of unknown possibilities in the day before me. These two women who had suddenly crossed my path, and their relations to the pale puffy-cheeked man at the little château, might well produce results more startling than had seemed to be offered even by such a freak as the original expedition undertaken by Gustave de Berensac and me. And now Gustave had fallen away and I was left to face the thing alone. For face it I must. My promise to the duchess bound me: had it not I doubt whether I should have gone; for my interest was not only in the duchess.

I had my coffee upstairs, and then, putting on my hat, went down for a stroll. So long as the duke did not come to Avranches, I could show my face boldly--and was not he busy preparing for his guests? I crossed the threshold of the hotel.

Just at the entrance stood Marie Delhasse; opposite her was a thickset fellow, neatly dressed and wearing mutton-chop whiskers. As I came out I raised my hat. The man appeared not to notice me, though his eyes fell on me for a moment. I passed quickly by--in fact, as quickly as I could--for it struck me at once that this man must be Lafleur, and I did not want him to give the duke a description of the unknown gentleman who was staying at Avranches. Yet, as I went, I had time to hear Marie's slow musical voice say:

"I'm not coming at all to-day."

I was very glad of it, and pursued my round of the town with a lighter heart. Presently, after half an hour's walk, I found myself opposite the church, and thus nearly back at the hotel: and in front of the church stood Marie Delhasse, looking at the façade.

Raising my hat I went up to her, her friendliness of the evening before encouraging me.

"I hope you are going to stay to-day?" said I.

"I don't know." Then she smiled, but not mirthfully. "I expect to be very much pressed to go this afternoon," she said.

I made a shot--apparently at a venture.

"Someone will come and carry you off?" I asked jestingly.

"It's very likely. My presence here will be known."

"But need you go?"

She looked on the ground and made no answer.

"Perhaps though," I continued, "he--or she--will not come. He may be too much occupied."

"To come for me?" she said, with the first touch of coquetry which I had seen in her lighting up her eyes.

"Even for that, it is possible," I rejoined.

We began to walk together toward the edge of the open *place* in front of the church. The convent came in sight as we reached the fall of the hill.

"How peaceful that looks!" she said; "I wonder if it would be pleasant there!"

I was myself just wondering how the Duchess of Saint-Maclou found it, when a loud cry of warning startled us. We had been standing on the edge of the road, and a horse, going at a quick trot, was within five yards of us. As it reached us, it was sharply reined in. To my amazement, old Jean, the duchess' servant, sat upon it. When he saw me, a smile spread over his weather-beaten face.

"I was nearly over you," said he. "You had no ears."

And I am sorry to say that Jean winked, insinuating that Marie Delhasse and I had been preoccupied.

The diplomacy of non-recognition had failed to strike Jean. I made the best of a bad job, and asked:

"What brings you here?"

Marie stood a few paces off, regarding us.

"I'm looking for Mme. la Duchesse," grinned Jean.

Marie Delhasse took a step forward when she heard his reference to the duchess.

"Her absence was discovered by Suzanne at six o'clock this morning," the old fellow went on. "And the duke--ah, take care how you come near him, sir! Oh, it's a kettle of fish! For as I came I met that coxcomb Lafleur riding back with a message from the duke's guests that they would not come to-day! So the duchess is gone, and the ladies are not come; and the duke--he has nothing to do but curse that whippersnapper of a Pierre who came last night."

And Jean ended in a rapturous hoarse chuckle.

"You were riding so fast, then, because you were after the duchess?" I suggested.

"I rode fast for fear," said Jean, with a shrewd smile, "that I should stop somewhere on the road. Well, I have looked in Avranches. She is not in Avranches. I'll go home again."

Marie Delhasse came close to my side.

"Ask him," she said to me, "if he speaks of the Duchess of Saint-Maclou."

I put the question as I was directed.

"You couldn't have guessed better if you'd known," said Jean; and a swift glance from Marie Delhasse told me that her suspicion as to my knowledge was aroused.

"And what will happen, Jean?" said I.

"The good God knows," shrugged Jean. Then, remembering perhaps my five-franc pieces, he said politely, "I hope you are well, sir?"

"Up to now, thank you, Jean," said I.

His glance traveled to Marie. I saw his shriveled lips curl; his expression was ominous of an unfortunate remark.

"Good-by!" said I significantly.

Jean had some wits. He spared me the remark, but not the sly leer that had been made to accompany it. He clapped his heels to his horse's side and trotted off in the direction from which he had come. So that he could swear he had been to

Avranches, he was satisfied!

Marie Delhasse turned to me, asking haughtily:

"What is the meaning of this? What do you know of the Duke or Duchess of Saint-Maclou?"

"I might return your question," said I, looking her in the face.

"Will you answer it?" she said, flushing red.

"No, Mlle. Delhasse, I will not," said I.

"What is the meaning of this 'absence' of the Duchess of Saint-Maclou which that man talks about so meaningly?"

Then I said, speaking low and slow:

"Who are the friends whom you are on your way to visit?"

"Who are you?" she cried. "What do you know about it? What concern is it of yours?"

There was no indolence or lack of animation in her manner now. She questioned me with imperious indignation.

"I will answer not a single word," said I. "But--you asked me last night what I had heard of you."

"Well?" she said, and shut her lips tightly on the word.

I held my peace; and in a moment she went on passionately:

"Who would have guessed that you would insult me? Is it your habit to insult women?"

"Not mine only, it seems," said I, meeting her glance boldly.

"What do you mean, sir?"

"Had you, then, an invitation from Mme. de Saint-Maclou?"

She drew back as if I had struck her. And I felt as though I had struck her. She looked at me for a moment with parted lips; then, without a word or a sign, she turned and walked slowly away in the direction of the hotel.

And I, glad to have something else to occupy my thoughts, started at a brisk pace along the foot-path that runs down the hill and meets the road which would lead me to the convent, for I had a thing or two to say to the duchess. And yet it was not of the duchess only that I thought as I went. There were also in my mind the indignant pride with which Marie Delhasse had questioned me, and the shrinking shame in her eyes at that counter-question of mine. The Duke of Saint-Maclou's invitation seemed to bring as much disquiet to one of his guests as it had to his wife herself. But one thing struck me, and I found a sort of comfort in it: she had thought, it seemed, that the duchess was to be at home.

"Pah!" I cried suddenly to myself. "If she weren't pretty, you'd say that made it worse!"

And I went on in a bad temper.

CHAPTER VII.
Heard through the Door.

Twenty minutes' walking brought me to the wood which lay between the road and the convent. I pressed on; soon the wood ceased and I found myself on the outskirts of a paddock of rough grass, where a couple of cows and half a dozen goats were pasturing; a row of stunted apple trees ran along one side of the paddock, and opposite me rose the white walls of the convent; while on my left was the burying-ground with its arched gateway, inscribed "Mors janua vitæ." I crossed the grass and rang a bell, that clanged again and again in echo. Nobody came. I pulled a second time and more violently. After some further delay the door was cautiously opened a little way, and a young woman looked out. She was a round-faced, red-cheeked, fresh creature, arrayed in a large close-fitting white cap, a big white collar over her shoulders, and a black gown. When she saw me, she uttered an exclamation of alarm, and pushed the door to again. Just in time I inserted my foot between door and doorpost.

"I beg your pardon," said I politely, "but you evidently misunderstand me. I wish to enter."

She peered at me through the two-inch gap my timely foot had preserved.

"But it is impossible," she objected. "Our rules do not allow it. Indeed, I may not talk to you. I beg of you to move your foot."

"But then you would shut the door."

She could not deny it.

"I mean no harm," I protested.

"'The guile of the wicked is infinite,'" remarked the little nun.

"I want to see the Mother Superior," said I. "Will you take my name to her?"

I heard another step in the passage. The door was flung wide open, and a stout and stately old lady faced me, a frown on her brow.

"Madame," said I, "until you hear my errand you will think me an ill-mannered fellow."

"What is your business, sir?"

"It is for your ear alone, madame."

"You can't come in here," said she decisively.

For a moment I was at a loss. Then the simplest solution in the world occurred to me.

"But you can come out, madame," I suggested.

She looked at me doubtfully for a minute. Then she stepped out, shutting the door carefully behind her. I caught a glimpse of the little nun's face, and thought there was a look of disappointment on it. The old lady and I began to walk along the path that led to the burying-ground.

"I do not know," said I, "whether you have heard of me. My name is Aycon."

"I thought so. Mr. Aycon, I must tell you that you are very much to blame. You have led this innocent, though thoughtless, child into most deplorable conduct."

("Well done, little duchess!" said I to myself; but of course I was not going to betray her.)

"I deeply regret my thoughtlessness," said I earnestly. "I would, however, observe that the present position of the duchess is not due to my--shall we say misconduct?--but to that of her husband. I did not invite--"

"Don't mention her name!" interrupted the Mother Superior in horror.

We had reached the arched gateway; and there appeared standing within it a figure most charmingly inappropriate to a graveyard--the duchess herself, looking as fresh as a daisy, and as happy as a child with a new toy. She ran to me, holding out both hands and crying:

"Ah, my dear, dear Mr. Aycon, you are the most delightful man alive! You come at the very moment I want you."

"Be sober, my child, be sober!" murmured the old lady.

"But I want to hear," expostulated the duchess. "Do you know anything, Mr. Aycon? What has been happening up at the house? What has the duke done?"

As the duchess poured out her questions, we passed through the gate; the ladies sat down on a stone bench just inside, and I, standing, told my story. The duchess was amused to hear of old Jean's chase of her; but she showed no astonishment till I told her that Marie Delhasse was at the hotel in Avranches, and had declined to go further on her journey to-day.

"At the hotel? Then you've seen her?" she burst out. "What is she like?"

"She is most extremely handsome," said I. "Moreover, I am inclined to like her."

The Mother Superior opened her lips--to reprove me, no doubt; but the duchess was too quick.

"Oh, you like her? Perhaps you're going to desert me and go over to her?" she cried in indignation, that was, I think, for the most part feigned. Certainly the duchess did not look very alarmed. But in regard to what she said, the old lady was bound to have a word.

"What is Mr. Aycon to you, my child?" said she solemnly. "He is nothing--nothing at all to you, my child."

"Well, I want him to be less than nothing to Mlle. Delhasse," said the duchess, with a pout for her protector and a glance for me.

"Mlle. Delhasse is very angry with me just now," said I.

"Oh, why?" asked the duchess eagerly.

"Because she gathered that I thought she ought to wait for an invitation from you, before she went to your house."

"She should wait till the Day of Judgment!" cried the duchess.

"That would not matter," observed the Mother Superior dryly.

Suddenly, without pretext or excuse, the duchess turned and walked very quickly--nay, she almost ran--away along the path that encircled the group of graves. Her eye had bidden me, and I followed no less briskly. I heard a despairing sigh from the poor old lady, but she had no chance of overtaking us. The audacious movement was successful.

"Now we can talk," said the duchess.

And talk she did, for she threw at me the startling assertion:

"I believe you're falling in love with Mlle. Delhasse. If you do, I'll never speak to you again!"

"If I do," said I, "I shall probably accept that among the other disadvantages of the entanglement."

"That's very rude," observed the duchess.

"Nothing with an 'if' in it is rude," said I speciously.

"Men must be always in love with somebody," said she resentfully.

"It certainly approaches a necessity," I assented.

The duchess glanced at me. Perhaps I had glanced at her; I hope not.

"Oh, well," said she, "hadn't we better talk business?"

"Infinitely better," said I; and I meant it.

"What am I to do?" she asked, with a return to her more friendly manner.

"Nothing," said I.

It is generally the safest advice--to women at all events.

"You are content with the position? You like being at the hotel perhaps?"

"Should I not be hard to please, if I didn't?"

"I know you are trying to annoy me, but you shan't. Mr. Aycon, suppose my husband comes over to Avranches, and sees you?"

"I have thought of that."

"Well, what have you decided?"

"Not to think about it till it happens. But won't he be thinking more about you than me?"

"He won't do anything about me," she said. "In the first place, he will want no scandal. In the second, he does not want me. But he will come over to see her."

"Her" was, of course, Marie Delhasse. The duchess assigned to her the sinister distinction of the simple pronoun.

"Surely he will take means to get you to go back?" I exclaimed.

"If he could have caught me before I got here, he would have been glad. Now he will wait; for if he came here and claimed me, what he proposed to do would become known."

There seemed reason in this; the duchess calculated shrewdly.

"In fact," said I, "I had better go back to the hotel."

"That does not seem to vex you much."

"Well, I can't stay here, can I?" said I, looking round at the nunnery. "It would be irregular, you know."

"You might go to another hotel," suggested she.

"It is most important that I should watch what is going on at my present hotel," said I gravely; for I did not wish to move.

"You are the most--" began the duchess.

But this bit of character-reading was lost. Slow but sure, the Mother Superior was at our elbows.

"Adieu, Mr. Aycon," said she.

I felt sure that she must manage the nuns admirably.

"Adieu!" said I, as though there was nothing else to be said.

"Adieu!" said the duchess, as though she would have liked to say something else.

And all in a moment I was through the gateway and crossing the paddock. But the duchess ran to the gate, crying:

"Mind you come again to-morrow!"

My expedition consumed nearly two hours; and one o'clock struck from the tower of the church as I slowly climbed the hill, feeling (I must admit it) that the rest of the day would probably be rather dull. Just as I reached the top, however, I came plump on Mlle. Delhasse, who appeared to be taking a walk. She bowed to me slightly and coldly. Glad that she was so distant (for I did not like her looks), I returned her salute, and pursued my way to the hotel. In the porch of it stood the waiter--my friend who had taken such an obliging view of my movements the night before. Directly he saw me, he came out into the road to meet me.

"Are you acquainted with the ladies who have rooms on the first floor?" he asked with an air of mystery.

"I met them here for the first time," said I.

I believe he doubted me; perhaps waiters are bred to suspicion by the things they see.

"Ah!" said he, "then it does not interest you to know that a gentleman has been to see the young lady?"

I took out ten francs.

"Yes, it does," said I, handing him the money. "Who was it?"

"The Duke of Saint-Maclou," he whispered mysteriously.

"Is he gone?" I asked in some alarm. I had no wish to encounter him.

"This half-hour, sir."

"Did he see both the ladies?"

"No; only the young lady. Madame went out immediately on his arrival, and is not yet returned."

"And mademoiselle?"

"She is in her room."

Thinking I had not got much, save good will, for my ten francs--for he told me nothing but what I had expected to hear--I was about to pass on, when he added, in a tone which seemed more significant than the question demanded:

"Are you going up to your room, sir?"

"I am," said I.

"Permit me to show you the way," he said--though his escort seemed to me very unnecessary.

He mounted before me. We reached the first floor. Opposite to us, not three yards away, was the door of the sitting-room which I knew to be occupied by the Delhasses.

"Go on," said I.

"In a moment, sir," he said.

Then he held up his hand in the attitude of a man who listens.

"One should not listen," he whispered, apologetically; "but it is so strange. I thought that if you knew the lady--Hark!"

I knew that we ought not to listen. But the mystery of the fellow's manner and the concern of his air constrained me, and I too paused, listening.

From behind the door there came to our strained attentive ears the sound of a woman sobbing. I sought the waiter's eyes; they were already bent on me. Again the sad sounds came--low, swift, and convulsive. It went to my heart to hear them. I did not know what to do. To go on upstairs to my own room and mind my own business seemed the simple thing--simple, easy, and proper. But my feet were glued to the boards. I could not go, with that sound beating on my ears: I should hear it all the day. I glanced again at the waiter. He was a kind-looking fellow, and I saw the tears standing in his eyes.

"And mademoiselle is so beautiful!" he whispered.

"What the devil business is it of yours?" said I, in a low but fierce tone.

"None," said he. "I am content to leave it to you, sir;" and without more he turned and went downstairs.

It was all very well to leave it to me; but what--failing that simple, easy, proper, and impossible course of action which I have indicated--was I to do?

Well, what I did was this: I went to the door of the room and knocked softly. There was no answer. The sobs continued. I had been a brute to this girl in the morning; I thought of that as I stood outside.

"My God! what's the matter with her?" I whispered.

And then I opened the door softly.

Marie Delhasse sat in a chair, her head resting in her hands and her hands on the table; and her body was shaken with her weeping.

And on the table, hard by her bowed golden head, there lay a square leathern box. I stood on the threshold and looked at her.

The rest of the day did not now seem likely to be dull; but it might prove to have in store for me more difficult tasks than the enduring of a little dullness.

CHAPTER VIII.
I Find that I Care.

For a moment I stood stock still, wishing to Heaven that I had not opened the door; for I could find now no excuse for my intrusion, and no reason why I should not have minded my own business. The impulse that had made the thing done was exhausted in the doing of it. Retreat became my sole object; and, drawing back, I pulled the door after me. But I had given Fortune a handle--very literally; for the handle of the door grated loud as I turned it. Despairing of escape, I stood still. Marie Delhasse looked up with a start.

"Who's there?" she cried in frightened tones, hastily pressing her handkerchief to her eyes.

There was no help for it. I stepped inside, saying:

"I'm ashamed to say that I am."

I deserved and expected an outburst of indignation. My surprise was great when she sank against the back of the chair with a sigh of relief. I lingered awkwardly just inside the threshold.

"What do you want? Why did you come in?" she asked, but rather in bewilderment than anger.

"I was passing on my way upstairs, and--and you seemed to be in distress."

"Did I make such a noise as that?" said she. "I'm as bad as a child; but children cry because they mustn't do things, and I because I must."

We appeared to be going to talk. I shut the door.

"My intrusion is most impertinent," said I. "You have every right to resent it."

"Oh, have I the right to resent anything? Did you think so this morning?" she asked impetuously.

"The morning," I observed, "is a terribly righteous time with me. I must beg your pardon for what I said."

"You think the same still?" she retorted quickly.

"That is no excuse for having said it," I returned. "It was not my affair."

"It is nobody's affair, I suppose, but mine."

"Unless you allow it to be," said I. I could not endure the desolation her words and tone implied.

She looked at me curiously.

"I don't understand," she said in a fretfully weary tone, "how you come to be mixed up in it at all."

"It's a long story." Then I went on abruptly: "You thought it was someone else that had entered."

"Well, if I did?"

"Someone returning," said I stepping up to the table opposite her.

"What then?" she asked, but wearily and not in the defiant manner of the morning.

"Mme. Delhasse perhaps, or perhaps the Duke of Saint-Maclou?"

Marie Delhasse made no answer. She sat with her elbows on the table, and her chin resting on the support of her clenched hands; her lids drooped over her eyes; and I could not see the expression of her glance, which was, nevertheless, upon me.

"Well, well," I continued, "we needn't talk about him. Have you been doing some shopping?" And I pointed to the red leathern box.

For full half a minute she sat, without speech or movement. Then she said in answer to my question, which she could not take as an idle one:

"Yes, I have been doing some bargaining."

"Is that the result?"

Again she paused long before she answered.

"That," said she, "is a trifle--thrown in."

"To bind the bargain?" I suggested.

"Yes, Mr. Aycon--to bind the bargain."

"Is it allowed to look?"

"I think everything must be allowed to you. You would be so surprised if it were not."

I understood that she was aiming a satirical remark at me: I did not mind that; she had better flay me alive than sit and cry.

"Then I may open the box?"

"The key is in it."

I drew the box across, and I took a chair that stood by. I turned the key of the box. A glance showed me Marie's drooped lids half raised and her eyes fixed on my face.

I opened the box: there lay in it, in sparkling coil on the blue velvet, a magnificent diamond necklace; one great stone formed a pendent, and it was on this stone that I fixed my regard. I took it up and looked at it closely; then I examined the necklace itself. Marie's eyes followed my every motion.

"You like these trinkets?" I asked.

"Yes," said she, in that tone in which "yes" is stronger than a thousand words of rapture; and the depths of her eyes caught fire from the stones, and gleamed.

"But you know nothing about them," I pursued composedly.

"I suppose they are valuable," said she, making an effort after *nonchalance*.

"They have some value," I conceded, smiling. "But I mean about their history."

"They are bought, I suppose--bought and sold."

"I happen to know just a little about such things. In fact, I have a book at home in which there is a picture of this necklace. It is known as the Cardinal's Necklace. The stones were collected by Cardinal Armand de Saint-Maclou, Archbishop of Caen, some thirty years ago. They were set by Lebeau of Paris, on the order of the cardinal, and were left by him to his nephew, our friend the duke. Since his marriage, the duchess has of course worn them."

All this I said in a most matter-of-fact tone.

"Do you mean that they belong to her?" asked Marie, with a sudden lift of her eyes.

"I don't know. Strictly, I should think not," said I impassively.

Marie Delhasse stretched out her hand and began to finger the stones.

"She wore them, did she?"

"Certainly."

"Ah! I supposed they had just been bought." And she took her fingers off them.

"It would take a large sum to do that--to buy them *en bloc*," I observed.

"How much?"

"Oh, I don't know! The market varies so much: perhaps a million francs, per-haps more. You can't tell how much people will give for such things."

"No, it is difficult," she assented, again fingering the necklace, "to say what people will give for them."

I leaned back in my chair. There was a pause. Then her eyes suddenly met mine again, and she exclaimed defiantly:

"Oh, you know very well what it means! What's the good of fencing about it?"

"Yes, I know what it means," said I. "When have you promised to go?"

"To-morrow," she answered.

"Because of this thing?" and I pointed to the necklace.

"Because of--How dare you ask me such questions!"

I rose from my seat and bowed.

"You are going?" she asked, her fingers on the necklace, and her eyes avoiding mine.

"I have the honor," said I, "to enjoy the friendship of the Duchess of Saint-Maclou."

"And that forbids you to enjoy mine?"

I bowed assent to her inference. She sat still at the table, her chin on her hands. I was about to leave her, when it struck me all in a moment that leaving her was not exactly the best thing to do, although it might be much the easiest. I arrested my steps.

"Well," she asked, "is not our acquaintance ended?"

And she suddenly opened her hands and hid her face in them. It was a strange conclusion to a speech so coldly and distantly begun.

"For God's sake, don't go!" said I, bending a little across the table toward her.

"What's it to you? What's it to anybody?" came from between her fingers.

"Your mother--" I began.

She dropped her hands from her face, and laughed. It was a laugh the like of which I hope not to hear again. Then she broke out:

"Why wouldn't she have me in the house? Why did she run away? Am I unfit to touch her?"

"If she were wrong, you're doing your best to make her right."

"If everybody thinks one wicked, one may as well be wicked, and--and live in peace."

"And get diamonds?" I added, "Weren't you wicked?"

"No," she said, looking me straight in the face. "But what difference did that make?"

"None at all, in one point of view," said I. But to myself I was swearing that she should not go.

Then she said in a very low tone:

"He never leaves me. Ah! he makes everyone think--"

"Let 'em think," said I.

"If everyone thinks it--"

"Oh, come, nonsense!" said I.

"You know what you thought. What honest woman would have anything to do with me--or what honest man either?"

I had nothing to say about that; so I said again.

"Well, don't go, anyhow."

She spoke in lower tones, as she answered this appeal of mine:

"I daren't refuse. He'll be here again; and my mother--"

"Put it off a day or two," said I. "And don't take that thing."

She looked at me, it seemed to me, in astonishment.

"Do you really care?" she asked, speaking very low.

I nodded. I did care, somehow.

"Enough to stand by me, if I don't go?"

I nodded again.

"I daren't refuse right out. My mother and he--"

She broke off.

"Have something the matter with you: flutters or something," I suggested.

The ghost of a smile appeared on her face.

"You'll stay?" she asked.

I had to stay, anyhow. Perhaps I ought to have said so, and not stolen credit;

but all I did was to nod again.

"And, if I ask you, you'll--you'll stand between me and him?"

I hoped that my meeting with the duke would not be in a strong light; but I only said:

"Rather! I'll do anything I can, of course."

She did not thank me; she looked at me again. Then she observed.

"My mother will be back soon."

"And I had better not be here?"

"No."

I advanced to the table again, and laid my hand on the box containing the Cardinal's necklace.

"And this?" I asked in a careless tone.

"Ought I to send them back?"

"You don't want to?"

"What's the use of saying I do? I love them. Besides, he'll see through it. He'll know that I mean I won't come. I daren't--I daren't show him that!"

Then I made a little venture; for, fingering the box idly, I said:

"It would be uncommonly handsome of you to give 'em to the duchess."

"To the duchess?" she gasped in wondering tones.

"You see," I remarked, "either they are the duchess', in which case she ought to have them; or, if they were the duke's, they're yours now; and you can do what you like with them."

"He gave them me on--on a condition."

"A condition," said I, "no gentleman could mention, and no law enforce."

She blushed scarlet, but sat silent.

"Revenge is sweet," said I. "She ran away rather than meet you. You send her her diamonds!"

A sudden gleam shot into Marie Delhasse's eyes.

"Yes," she said, "yes." And stopped, thinking, with her hands clasped.

"You send them by me," I pursued, delighted with the impression which my suggestion had made upon her.

"By you? You see her, then?" she asked quickly.

"Occasionally," I answered. The duchess' secret was not mine, and I did not say where I saw her.

"I'll give them to you," said Marie--"to you, not to the duchess."

"I won't have 'em at any price," said I. "Come, your mother will be back soon. I believe you want to keep 'em." And I assumed a disgusted air.

"I don't!" she flashed out passionately. "I don't want to touch them! I wouldn't keep them for the world!"

I looked at my watch. With a swift motion, Marie Delhasse leaped from her chair, dashed down the lid of the box, hiding the glitter of the stones, seized the box in her two hands and with eyes averted held it out to me.

"For the duchess?" I asked.

"Yes, for the duchess," said Marie, with, averted eyes.

I took the box, and stowed it in the capacious pocket of the shooting-jacket which I was wearing.

"Go!" said Marie, pointing to the door.

I held out my hand. She caught it in hers. Upon my word, I thought she was going to kiss it. So strongly did I think it that, hating fuss of that sort, I made a half-motion to pull it away. However, I was wrong. She merely pressed it and let it drop.

"Cheer up! cheer up! I'll turn up again soon," said I, and I left the room.

And left in the nick of time; for at the very moment when I, hugging the lump in my coat which marked the position of the Cardinal's Necklace, reached the foot of the stairs Mme. Delhasse appeared on her way up.

"Oh, you old viper!" I murmured thoughtlessly, in English.

"Pardon, monsieur?" said Mme. Delhasse.

"Forgive me: I spoke to myself--a foolish habit," I rejoined, with a low bow and, I'm afraid, a rather malicious smile. The old lady glared at me, bobbed her head the slightest bit in the world, and passed me by.

I went out into the sunshine, whistling merrily. My good friend the waiter stood by the door. His eyes asked me a question.

"She is much better," I said reassuringly. And I walked out, still whistling merrily.

In truth I was very pleased with myself. Every man likes to think that he understands women. I was under the impression that I had proved myself to possess a thorough and complete acquaintance with that intricate subject. I was soon to find that my knowledge had its limitations. In fact, I have been told more than once since that my plan was a most outrageous one. Perhaps it was; but it had the effect of wresting those dangerous stones from poor Marie's regretful hands. A man need not mind having made a fool of himself once or twice on his way through the world, so he has done some good by the process. At the moment, however, I felt no need for any such apology.

CHAPTER IX.
An Unparalleled Insult.

I was thoughtful as I walked across the ***place*** in front of the church in the full glare of the afternoon sun. It was past four o'clock; the town was more lively, as folk, their day's work finished, came out to take their ease and filled the streets and the cafés. I felt that I also had done something like a day's work; but my task was not complete till I had lodged my precious trust safely in the keeping of the duchess.

There was, however, still time to spare, and I sat down at a café and ordered some coffee. While it was being brought my thoughts played round Marie Delhasse. I doubted whether I disliked her for being tempted, or liked her for resisting at the last; at any rate, I was glad to have helped her a little. If I could now persuade her to leave Avranches, I should have done all that could reasonably be expected of me; if the duke pursued, she must fight the battle for herself. So I mused, sipping my coffee; and then I fell to wondering what the duchess would say on seeing me again so soon. Would she see me? She must, whether she liked it or not; I could not keep the diamonds all night. Perhaps she would like.

"There you are again!" I said to myself sharply, and I roused myself from my meditations.

As I looked up, I saw the man Lafleur opposite to me. He had his back toward me, but I knew him, and he was just walking into a shop that faced the café and displayed in its windows an assortment of offensive weapons--guns, pistols, and various sorts of knives. Lafleur went in. I sat sipping my coffee. He was there nearly twenty minutes; then he came out and walked leisurely away. I paid my score and strolled over to the shop. I wondered what he had been buying. Dueling pistols for the duke, perhaps! I entered and asked to be shown some penknives. The shopman served me with alacrity. I chose a cheap knife, and then I permitted my gaze to rest on a neat little pistol that lay on the counter. My simple *ruse* was most effective. In a moment I was being acquainted with all the merits of the instrument, and the eulogy was backed by the information that a gentleman had bought two pistols of the same make not ten minutes before I entered the shop.

"Really!" said I. "What for?"

"Oh, I don't know, sir. It is a wise thing often to carry one of these little fellows. One never knows."

"In case of a quarrel with another gentleman?"

"Oh, they are hardly such as we sell for dueling, sir."

"Aren't they?"

"They are rather pocket pistols--to carry if you are out at night; and we sell many to gentlemen who have occasion in the way of their business to carry large sums of money or valuables about with them. They give a sense of security, sir, even if no occasion arises for their use."

"And this gentleman bought two? Who was he?"

"I don't know, sir. He gave me no name."

"And you didn't know him by sight?"

"No, sir; perhaps he is a stranger. But indeed I'm almost that myself: I have but just set up business here."

"Is it brisk?" I asked, examining the pistol.

"It is not a brisk place, sir," the man answered regretfully. "Let me sell you one, sir!"

It happened to be, for the moment, in the way of my business to carry valuables, but I hoped it would not be for long, so that I did not buy a pistol; but I allowed myself to wonder what my friend Lafleur wanted with two--and they were not dueling pistols! If I had been going to keep the diamonds--but then I was not. And, reminded by this reflection, I set out at once for the convent.

Now the manner in which the Duchess of Saint-Maclou saw fit to treat me--who was desirous only of serving her--on this occasion went far to make me disgusted with the whole affair into which I had been drawn. It might have been supposed that she would show gratitude; I think that even a little admiration and a little appreciation of my tact would not have been, under the circumstances, out of place. It is not every day that a lady has such a thing as the Cardinal's Necklace res-cued from great peril and freely restored, with no claim (beyond that for ordinary civility) on the part of the rescuer.

And the cause did not lie in her happening to be out of temper, for she greeted me at first with much graciousness, and sitting down on the corn bin (she was permitted on this occasion to meet me in the stable), she began to tell me that she had received a most polite--and indeed almost affectionate--letter from the duke, in which he expressed deep regret for her absence, but besought her to stay where she was as long as the health of her soul demanded. He would do himself the honor of waiting on her and escorting her home, when she made up her mind to return to him.

"Which means," observed the duchess, as she replaced the letter in her pocket, "that the Delhasses are going, and that if I go (without notice anyhow) I shall find them there."

"I read it in the same way; but I'm not so sure that the Delhasses are going."

"You are so charitable," said she, still quite sweetly. "You can't bring yourself to think evil of anybody."

The duchess chanced to look so remarkably calm and composed as she sat on the corn bin that I could not deny myself the pleasure of surprising her with the sudden apparition of the Cardinal's Necklace. Without a word, I took the case out of my pocket, opened it, and held it out toward her. For once the duchess sat stock-still, her eyes round and large.

"Have you been robbing and murdering my husband?" she gasped.

With a very complacent smile I began my story. Who does not know what it is to begin a story with a triumphant confidence in its favorable reception? Who does not know that first terrible glimmer of doubt when the story seems not to be making the expected impression? Who has not endured the dull dogged despair in which the story, damned by the stony faces of the auditors, has yet to drag on a hated weary life to a dishonored grave?

These stages came and passed as I related to Mme. de Saint-Maclou how I came to be in a position to hand back to her the Cardinal's Necklace. Still, silent, pale, with her lips curled in a scornful smile, she sat and listened. My tone lost its trium-phant ring, and I finished in cold, distant, embarrassed accents.

"I have only," said I, "to execute my commission and hand the box and its contents over to you."

And, thus speaking, I laid the necklace in its case on the corn bin beside the duchess.

The duchess said nothing at all. She looked at me once--just once; and I wished then and there that I had listened to Gustave de Berensac's second thoughts and left with him at ten o'clock in the morning. Then having delivered this barbed shaft of the eyes, the duchess sat looking straight in front of her, bereft of her quick-changing glances, robbed of her supple grace--like frozen quicksilver. And the necklace glittered away indifferently between us.

At last the duchess, her eyes still fixed on the whitewashed wall opposite, said in a slow emphatic tone:

"I wouldn't touch it, if it were the crown of France!"

I plucked up my courage to answer her. For Marie Delhasse's sake I felt a sudden anger.

"You are pharisaical," said I. "The poor girl has acted honorably. Her touch has not defiled your necklace."

"Yes, you must defend what you persuaded," flashed out the duchess. "It's the greatest insult I was ever subjected to in my life!"

Here was the second lady I had insulted on that summer day!

"I did but suggest it--it was her own wish."

"Your suggestion is her wish! How charming!" said the duchess.

"You are unjust to her!" I said, a little warmly.

The duchess rose from the corn bin, made the very most of her sixty-three inches, and remarked:

"It's a new insult to mention her to me."

I passed that by; it was too absurd to answer.

"You must take it now I've brought it," I urged in angry puzzle.

The duchess put out her hand, grasped the case delicately, shut it--and flung it to the other side of the stable, hard by where an old ass was placidly eating a bundle of hay.

"That's the last time I shall touch it!" said she, turning and looking me in the face.

"But what am I to do with it?" I cried.

"Whatever you please," returned Mme. de Saint-Maclou; and without another word, without another glance, either at me or at the necklace, she walked out of the stable, and left me alone with the necklace and the ass.

The ass had given one start as the necklace fell with a thud on the floor; but he was old and wise, and soon fell again to his meal. I sat drumming my heels against the corn bin. Evening was falling fast, and everything was very still. No man ever had a more favorable hour for reflection and introspection. I employed it to the full. Then I rose, and crossing the stable, pulled the long ears of my friend who was eating the hay.

"I suppose you also were a young ass once," said I with a rueful smile.

Well, I couldn't leave the Cardinal's Necklace in the corner of the convent stable. I picked up the box. Neddy thrust out his nose at it. I opened it and let him see the contents. He snuffed scornfully and turned back to the hay.

"He won't take it either," said I to myself, and with a muttered curse I dropped the wretched thing back in the pocket of my coat, wishing much evil to everyone who had any hand in bringing me into connection with it, from his Eminence the Cardinal Armand de Saint-Maclou down to the waiter at the hotel.

Slowly and in great gloom of mind I climbed the hill again. I supposed that I must take the troublesome ornament back to Marie Delhasse, confessing that my fine idea had ended in nothing save a direct and stinging insult for her and a scathing snub for me. My pride made this necessity hard to swallow, but I believe there was also a more worthy feeling that caused me to shrink from it. I feared that her good resolutions would not survive such treatment, and that the rebuff would drive her headlong into the ruin from which I had trusted that she would be saved. Yet there was nothing else for it. Back the necklace must go. I could but pray--and earnestly I did pray--that my fears might not be realized.

I found myself opposite the gun-maker's shop; and it struck me that I might probably fail to see Marie alone that evening. I had no means of defense--I had never thought any necessary. But now a sudden nervousness got hold of me: it seemed to me as if my manner must betray to everyone that I carried the necklace--as if the lump in my coat stood out conspicuous as Mont St. Michel itself. Feeling that I was doing a half-absurd thing, still I stepped into the shop and announced that, on further reflection, I would buy the little pistol. The good man was delighted to sell it to me.

"If you carry valuables, sir," he said, repeating his stock recommendation, "it will give you a feeling of perfect safety."

"I don't carry valuables," said I abruptly, almost rudely, and with most unnecessary emphasis.

"I did but suggest, sir," he apologized. "And at least, it may be that you will require to do so some day."

"That," I was forced to admit, "is of course not impossible." And I slid the pistol and a supply of cartridges into the other pocket of my coat.

"Distribute the load, sir," advised the smiling nuisance. "One side of your coat will be weighed down. Ah, pardon! I perceive that there is already something in the other pocket."

"A sandwich-case," said I; and he bowed with exactly the smile the waiter had worn when I said that I came from Mont St. Michel.

CHAPTER X.
Left on my Hands.

There is nothing else for it!" I exclaimed, as I set out for the hotel. "I'll go back to England."

I could not resist the conclusion that my presence in Avranches was no longer demanded. The duchess had, on the one hand, arrived at a sort of understanding with her husband; while she had, on the other, contrived to create a very considerable misunderstanding with me. She had shown no gratitude for my efforts, and made no allowance for the mistakes which, possibly, I had committed. She had behaved so unreasonably as to release me from any obligation. As to Marie Delhasse, I had had enough (so I declared in the hasty disgust my temper engendered) of Quixotic endeavors to rescue people who, had they any moral resolution, could well rescue themselves. There was only one thing left which I might with dignity undertake--and that was to put as many miles as I could between the scene of my unappreciated labors and myself. This I determined to do the very next day, after handing back this abominable necklace with as little obvious appearance of absurdity as the action would permit.

It was six o'clock when I reached the hotel and walked straight up to my room in sulky isolation, looking neither to right nor left, and exchanging a word with nobody. I tossed the red box down on the table, and flung myself into an armchair. I had half a mind to send the box down to Marie Delhasse by the waiter--with my compliments; but my ill-humor did not carry me so far as thus to risk betraying her to her mother, and I perceived that I must have one more interview with her--and the sooner the better. I rang the bell, meaning to see if I could elicit from the waiter any information as to the state of affairs on the first floor and the prospect of finding Marie alone for ten minutes.

I rang once--twice--thrice; the third was a mighty pull, and had at last the effect of bringing up my friend the waiter, breathless, hot, and disheveled.

"Why do you keep me waiting like this?" I asked sternly.

His puffs and pants prevented him from answering for a full half-minute.

"I was busy on the first floor, sir," he protested at last. "I came at the very earliest moment."

"What's going on on the first floor?"

"The lady is in a great hurry, sir. She is going away, sir. She has been taking a hasty meal, and her carriage is ordered to be round at the door this very minute. And all the luggage had to be carried down, and--"

I walked to the window, and, putting my head out, saw a closed carriage, with four trunks and some smaller packages on the roof, standing at the door.

"Where are they going?" I asked, turning round.

The waiter was gone! A bell ringing violently from below explained his disappearance, but did not soothe my annoyance. I rang my bell very forcibly again: the action was a welcome vent for my temper. Turning back to the window, I found the carriage still there. A second or two later, Mme. Delhasse, attended by the waiter who ought to have been looking after me, came out of the hotel and got into the carriage. She spoke to the waiter, and appeared to give him money. He bowed and closed the door. The driver started his horses and made off at a rapid pace toward the carriage-road down the hill. I watched till the vehicle was out of sight and then drew my head in, giving a low puzzled whistle and forgetting the better part of my irritation in the interest of this new development. Where was the old witch going--and why was she going alone?

Again I rang my bell; but the waiter was at the door before it ceased tinkling.

"Where's she going to?" I asked.

"To the house of the Duke of Saint-Maclou, sir," he answered, wiping his brow and sighing for relief that he had got rid of her.

"And the young lady--where is she?"

"She has already gone, sir."

"Already gone!" I cried. "Gone where? Gone when?"

"About two hours ago, sir--very soon after I saw you go out, sir--a messenger brought a letter for the young lady. I took it upstairs; she was alone when I entered.

When she looked at the address, sir, she made a little exclamation, and tore the note open in a manner that showed great agitation. She read it; and when she had read it stood still, holding it in her hand for a minute or two. She had turned pale and breathed quickly. Then she signed to me with her hand to go. But she stopped me with another gesture, and--and then, sir--"

"Well, well, get on!" I cried.

"Then, sir, she asked if you were in the hotel, and I said no--you had gone out, I did not know where. Upon that, she walked to the window, and stood looking out for a time. Then she turned round to me, and said: 'My mother was fatigued by her walk, and is sleeping. I am going out, but I do not wish her disturbed. I will write a note of explanation. Be so good as to cause it to be given to her when she wakes.' She was calm then, sir; she sat down and wrote, and sealed the note and gave it to me. Then she caught up her hat, which lay on the table, and her gloves; and then, sir, she walked out of the hotel."

"Which way did she go?"

"She went, sir, as if she were making for the footpath down the hill. An hour or more passed, and then madame's bell rang. I ran up and, finding her in the sitting room, I gave her the note."

"And what did she say?"

"She read it, and cried 'Ah!' in great satisfaction, and immediately ordered a carriage and that the maid should pack all her luggage and the young lady's. Oh! she was in a great hurry, and in the best of spirits; and she pressed us on so that I was not able to attend properly to you, sir. And finally, as you saw, she drove off to the house of the duke, still in high good humor."

The waiter paused. I sat silent in thought.

"Is there anything else you wish to know, sir?" asked the waiter.

Then my much-tried temper gave way again.

"I want to know what the devil it all means!" I roared.

The waiter drew near, wearing a very sympathetic expression. I knew that he had always put me down as an admirer of Marie Delhasse. He saw in me now a beaten rival. Curiously I had something of the feeling myself.

"There is one thing, sir," said he. "The stable-boy told me. The message for Mlle. Delhasse was brought from a carriage which waited at the bottom of the hill, out of sight of the town. And--well, sir, the servants wore no livery; but the boy declares that the horses were those of the Duke of Saint-Maclou."

I muttered angrily to myself. The waiter, discreetly ignoring my words, continued:

"And, indeed, sir, madame expected to meet her daughter. For I chanced to ask her if she would take with her a bouquet of roses which she had purchased in the town, and she answered: 'Give them to me. My daughter will like to have them.'"

The waiter's conclusion was obvious. And yet I did not accept it. For why, if Marie were going to the duke's, should she not have aroused her mother and gone with her? That the duke had sent his carriage for her was likely enough; that he would cause it to wait outside the town was not impossible; that Marie had told her mother that she had gone to the duke's was also clear from that lady's triumphant demeanor. But that she had in reality gone, I could not believe. A sudden thought struck me.

"Did Mlle. Delhasse," I asked, "send any answer to the note that came from the carriage?"

"Ah, sir, I forgot. Certainly. She wrote an answer, and the messenger carried it away with him."

"And did the boy you speak of see anything more of the carriage?"

"He did not pass that way again, sir."

My mind was now on the track of Marie's device. The duke had sent his carriage to fetch her. She, left alone, unable to turn to me for guidance, determined not to go; afraid to defy him--more afraid, no doubt, because she could no longer produce the necklace--had played a neat trick. She must have sent a message to the duke that she would come with her mother immediately that the necessary preparations could be made; she had then written a note to her mother to tell her that she had gone in the duke's carriage and looked to her mother to follow her. And having thus thrown both parties on a false scent, she had put on her hat and walked quietly out of the hotel. But, then, where had she walked to? My chain of inference was broken by that missing link. I looked up at the waiter. And then I cursed my carelessness. For the waiter's eyes were no longer fixed on my face, but were fastened in eloquent curiosity on the red box which lay on my table. To my apprehensive fancy the Cardinal's Necklace seemed to glitter through the case. That did not of course happen; but a jewel case is easy to recognize, and I knew in a moment that the waiter discerned the presence of precious stones. Our eyes met. In my puzzle I could do nothing but smile feebly and apologetically. The waiter smiled also--but his was a smile of compassion and condolence. He took a step nearer to me, and with infinite sympathy in his tone observed:

"Ah, well, sir, do not despair! A gentleman like you will soon find another lady to value the present more."

In spite of my vanity--and I was certainly not presenting myself in a very triumphant guise to the waiter's imagination--I jumped at the mistake.

"They are capricious creatures!" said I with a shrug. "I'll trouble myself no more about them."

"You're right, sir, you're right. It's one one day, and another another. It's a pity, sir, to waste thought on them--much more, good money. You will dine to-night, sir?" and his tone took a consolatory inflection.

"Certainly I will dine," said I; and with a last nod of intelligence and commiseration, he withdrew.

And then I leaped, like a wildcat, on the box that contained the Cardinal's Necklace, intent on stowing it away again in the seclusion of my coat-pocket. But again I stood with it in my hand--struck still with the thought that I could not now return it to Marie Delhasse, that she had vanished leaving it on my hands, and that, in all likelihood, in three or four hours' time the Duke of Saint-Maclou would be scouring the country and setting every spring in motion in the effort to find the truant lady, and--what I thought he would be at least anxious about--the truant necklace. For to give your family heirlooms away without recompense is a vexatious thing; and ladies who accept them and vanish with them into space can claim but small consideration. And, moreover, if the missing property chance to be found in the possession of a gentleman who is reluctant to explain his presence, who has masqueraded as a groom with intent to deceive the owner of the said property, and has no visible business to bring or keep him on the spot at all--when all this happens, it is apt to look very awkward for that gentleman.

"You will regret it if you don't start with me;" so said Gustave de Berensac. The present was one of the moments in which I heartily agreed with his prescient prophecy. Human nature is a poor thing. To speak candidly, I cannot recollect that, amid my own selfish perplexities, I spared more than one brief moment to gladness that Marie Delhasse had eluded the pursuit of the Duke of Saint-Maclou. But I spared another to wishing that she had thought of telling me to what haven she was bound.

CHAPTER XI.
A Very Clever Scheme.

I must confess at once that I might easily have displayed more acumen, and that there would have been nothing wonderful in my discerning or guessing the truth about Marie Delhasse's movements. Yet the truth never occurred to me, never so much as suggested itself in the shape of a possible explanation. I cannot quite tell why; perhaps it conflicted too strongly with the idea of her which possessed me; perhaps it was characteristic of a temperament so different from my own that I could not anticipate it. At any rate, be the reason what it may, I did not seriously doubt that Marie Delhasse had cut the cords which bound her by a hasty flight from Avranches; and my conviction was deepened by my knowledge that an evening train left for Paris just about half an hour after Marie, having played her trick on her mother and on the Duke of Saint-Maclou, had walked out of the hotel, no man and no woman hindering her.

Under these circumstances, my work--imposed and voluntary alike--was done; and the cheering influence of the dinner to which I sat down so awoke my mind to fresh agility that I found the task of disembarrassing myself of that old man of the sea--the Cardinal's Necklace--no longer so hopeless as it had appeared in the hungry disconsolate hour before my meal. Nay, I saw my way to performing, incidentally, a final service to Marie by creating in the mind of the duke such chagrin and anger as would, I hoped, disincline him from any pursuit of her. If I could, by one stroke, restore him his diamonds and convince him, not of Marie's virtue, but of her faithlessness, I trusted to be humbly instrumental in freeing her from his importunity, and of restoring the jewels to the duchess--nay, of restoring to her also the undisturbed possession of her home and of the society of her husband. At this latter prospect I told myself that I ought to feel very satisfied, and rather to my surprise found myself feeling not very dissatisfied; for most unquestionably the duchess had treated me villainously and had entirely failed to appreciate me. My face still went hot to think of the glance she had given Marie Delhasse's maladroit ambassador.

After these reflections and a bottle of Burgundy (I will not apportion the credit) I rose from the table humming a tune and started to go upstairs, conning my scheme in a contented mind. As I passed through the hall the porter handed me a note, saying that a boy had left it and that there was no answer. I opened and read it; it was very short and it ran thus:

I wish never to see you again. ELSA.

Now "Elsa" (and I believe that I have not mentioned the fact before--an evidence, if any were needed, of my discretion) was the Christian name of the Duchess of Saint-Maclou. Picking up her dropped handkerchief as we rambled through the woods, I had seen the word delicately embroidered thereon, and I had not forgotten this chance information. But why--let those learned in the ways of women answer if they can--why, first, did she write at all? Why, secondly, did she tell me what had been entirely obvious from her demeanor? Why, thirdly, did she choose to affix to the document which put an end to our friendship a name which that friendship had never progressed far enough to justify me in employing? To none of these pertinent queries could I give a satisfactory reply. Yet, somehow, that "Elsa" standing alone, shorn of all aristocratic trappings, had a strange attraction for me, and carried with it a pleasure that the uncomplimentary tenor of the rest of the document did not entirely obliterate. "Elsa" wished never to see me again: that was bad; but it was "Elsa" who was so wicked as to wish that: that was good. And by a curious freak of the mind it occurred to me as a hardship that I had not received so much as a note of one line from--"Marie."

"Nonsense!" said I aloud and peevishly; and I thrust the letter into my pocket, cheek by jowl with the Cardinal's Necklace. And being thus vividly reminded of the presence of that undesired treasure, I became clearly resolved that I must not be arrested for theft merely because the Duchess of Saint-Maclou chose (from hurry, or carelessness, or what motive you will) to sign a disagreeable and unnecessary communication with her Christian name and nothing more, nor because Mlle. Delhasse chose to vanish without a word of civil farewell. Let them go their ways--I did not know which of them annoyed me more. Notwithstanding the letter, notwithstanding the disappearance, my scheme must be carried out. And then--for home! But the conclusion came glum and displeasing.

The scheme was very simple. I intended to spend the hours of the night in an excursion to the duke's house. I knew that old Jean slept in a detached cottage about half a mile from the château. Here I should find the old man. I would hand to him the necklace in its box, without telling him what the contents of the box were. Jean would carry the parcel to his master, and deliver with it a message to the effect that a gentleman who had left Avranches that afternoon had sent the parcel by a messenger to the duke, inasmuch as he had reason to believe that the article contained therein was the property of the duke and that the duke would probably be glad to have it restored to him. The significant reticence of this message was meant to inform the duke that Marie Delhasse was not so solitary in her flight but that she could find a cavalier to do her errands for her, and one who would not acquiesce in the retention of the diamonds. I imagined, with a great deal of pleasure, what the duke's feelings would be in face of the communication. Thus, then, the diamonds were to be restored, the duke disgusted, and I myself freed from all my troubles. I have often thought since that the scheme was really very ingenious, and showed a talent for intrigue which has been notably wanting in the rest of my humble career.

The scheme once prosperously carried through, I should, of course, take my departure at the earliest moment on the following day. I might, or I might not, write a line of dignified remonstrance to the duchess, but I should make no attempt to see her; and I should most certainly go. Moreover, it would be a long while before I accepted any of her harum-scarum invitations again.

"Elsa" indeed! Somehow I could not say it with quite the indignant scorn which I desired should be manifest in my tone. I have never been able to be indignant with the duchess; although I have laughed at her. Now I could be, and was, indignant with Marie Delhasse; though, in truth, her difficult position pleaded excuses for her treatment of me which the duchess could not advance.

As the clock of the church struck ten I walked downstairs from my room, wearing a light short overcoat tightly buttoned up. I informed the waiter that I was likely to be late, secured the loan of a latchkey, and left my good friend under the evident impression that I was about to range the shores of the bay in love-lorn solitude. Then I took the footpath down the hill and, swinging along at a round pace, was fairly started on my journey. If the inference I drew from the next thing I saw were correct, it was just as well for me to be out of the way for a little while. For, when I was still about thirty yards from the main road, there dashed past the end of the lane leading up the hill a carriage and pair, traveling at full speed. I could not see who rode inside; but two men sat on the box, and there was luggage on the top. I could not be sure in the dim light, but I had a very strong impression that the carriage was the same as that which had conveyed Mme. Delhasse out of my sight earlier in the evening. If it were so, and if the presence of the luggage indicated that of its owner, the good lady, arriving alone, must have met with the scantest welcome from the duke. And she would return in a fury of anger and suspicion. I was glad not to meet her; for if she were searching for explanation, I fancied, from glances she had given me, that I was likely to come in for a share of her attention. In fact, she might reasonably have supposed that I was interested in her daughter; nor, indeed, would she have been wrong so far.

Briskly I pursued my way, and in something over an hour I reached the turn in the road and, setting my face inland, began to climb the hill. A mile further on I came on a bypath, and not doubting from my memory of the direction, that this must be a short cut to the house, I left the road and struck along the narrow wooded track. But, although shorter than the road, it was not very direct, and I found myself thinking it very creditable to the topographical instinct of my friend and successor, Pierre, that he should have discovered on a first visit, and without having been to the house, that this was the best route to follow. With the knowledge of where the house lay, however, it was not difficult to keep right, and another forty minutes brought me, now creeping along very cautiously, alertly, and with open ears, to the door of old Jean's little cottage. No doubt he was fast asleep in his bed, and I feared the need of a good deal of noisy knocking before he could be awakened from a peasant's heavy slumber.

My delight was therefore great when I discovered that--either because he trusted his fellow-men, or because he possessed nothing in the least worth stealing--he had left his door simply on the latch. I lifted the latch and walked in. A dim lantern burned on a little table near the smoldering log-fire. Yet the light was enough to tell me that my involuntary host was not in the room. I passed across its short breadth to a door in the opposite wall. The door yielded to a push; all was dark inside. I listened for a sleeper's breathing, but heard nothing. I returned, took up the lantern, and carried it with me into the inner room. I held it above my head, and it enabled me to see the low pallet-bed in the corner. But Jean was not lying in the bed--nay, it was clear that he had not lain on the bed all that night. Yet his bedtime was half-past eight or nine, and it was now hard on one o'clock. Jean was "making a night of it," that seemed very clear. But what was the business or pleasure that engaged him? I admit that I was extremely annoyed. My darling scheme, on which I had prided myself so much, was tripped up by the trifling accident of Jean's absence.

What in the world, I asked again, kept the old man from his bed? It suddenly struck me that he might, by the duke's orders, have accompanied Mme. Delhasse back to Avranches, in order to be able to report to his master any news that came to light there. He might well have been the second man on the box. This reflection removed my surprise at his absence, but not my vexation. I did not know what to do! Should I wait? But he might not be back till morning. Wearily, in high disgust, I recognized that the great scheme had, for tonight at least, gone awry, and that I must tramp back to Avranches, carrying my old man of the sea, the Cardinal's Necklace. For Jean could not read, and it was useless to leave the parcel with written directions.

I went into the outer room, and set the lantern in its place; I took a pull at my flask, and smoked a pipe. Then, with a last sigh of vexation, I grasped my stick in my hand, rose to my feet, and moved toward the door.

Ah! Hark! There was a footstep outside.

"Thank Heaven, here comes the old fool!" I murmured.

The step came on, and, as it came, I listened to it; and as I listened to it, the sudden satisfaction that had filled me as suddenly died away; for, if that were the step of old Jean, may I see no difference between the footfalls of an elephant and of a ballet-dancer! And then, before I had time to form any plan, or to do anything save stand staring in the middle of the floor, the latch was lifted again, the door opened, and in walked--the Duke of Saint-Maclou!

CHAPTER XII.
As a Man Possessed.

The dim light served no further than to show that a man was there.

"Well, Jean, what news?" asked the duke, drawing the door close behind him.

"I am not Jean," said I.

"Then who the devil are you, and what are you doing here?" He advanced and held up the lantern. "Why, what are you hanging about for?" he exclaimed the next moment, with a start of surprise.

"And I am not George Sampson either," said I composedly. I had no mind to play any more tricks. As I must meet him, it should be in my own character.

The duke studied me from top to toe. He twirled his mustache, and a slight smile appeared on his full lips.

"Yet I know you as George Sampson, I think, sir," said he, but in an altered tone. He spoke now as though to an equal--to an enemy perhaps, but to an equal.

I was in some perplexity; but a moment later he relieved me.

"You need trouble yourself with no denials," he said. "Lafleur's story of the gentleman at Avranches, with the description of him, struck me as strange; and for the rest--there were two things."

He seated himself on a stool. I leaned against the wall.

"In the first place," he continued, "I know my wife pretty well; in the second, a secret known to four maidservants-- Really, sir, you were very confiding!"

"I was doing no wrong," said I; though not, I confess, in a very convinced tone.

"Then why the masquerade?" he answered quickly, hitting my weak point.

"Because you were known to be unreasonable."

His smile broadened a little.

"It's the old crime of husbands, isn't it?" he asked. "Well, sir, I'm no lawyer, and it's not my purpose to question you on that matter. I will put you to no denials."

I bowed. The civility of his demeanor was a surprise to me.

"If that were the only affair, I need not keep you ten minutes," he went on. "At least, I presume that my friend would find you when he wanted to deliver a message from me?"

"Certainly. But may I ask why, if that is your intention, you have delayed so long? You guessed I was at Avranches. Why not have sent to me?"

The duke tugged his mustache.

"I do not know your name, sir," he remarked.

"My name is Aycon."

"I know the name," and he bowed slightly. "Well, I didn't send to you at Avranches because I was otherwise occupied."

"I am glad, sir, that you take it so lightly," said I.

"And by the way, Mr. Aycon, before you question me, isn't there a question I might ask you? How came you here to-night?" And, as he spoke, his smile vanished.

"I have nothing to say, beyond that I hoped to see your servant Jean."

"For what purpose? Come, sir, for what purpose? I have a right to ask for what purpose." And his tone rose in anger.

I was going to give him a straightforward answer. My hand was actually on the way to the spot where I felt the red box pressing against my side, when he rose from his seat and strode toward me; and a sudden passion surged in his voice.

"Answer me! answer me!" he cried. "No, I'm not asking about my wife; I don't care a farthing for that empty little parrot. Answer me, sir, as you value your life! What do you know of Marie Delhasse?"

And he stood before me with uplifted hand, as though he meant to strike me. I did not move, and we looked keenly into one another's eyes. He controlled himself by a great effort, but his hands trembled, as he continued:

"That old hag who came to-night and dared to show her filthy face here without her daughter--she told me of your talks and walks. The girl was ready to come. Who stopped her? Who turned her mind? Who was there but you--you--you?"

And again his passion overcame him, and he was within an ace of dashing his fist in my face.

My hands hung at my side, and I leaned easily against the wall.

"Thank God," said I, "I believe I stopped her! I believe I turned her mind. I did my best, and except me, nobody was there."

"You admit it?"

"I admit the crime you charged me with. Nothing more."

"What have you done with her? Where is she now?"

"I don't know."

"Ah!" he cried, in angry incredulity. "You don't know, don't you?"

"And if I knew, I wouldn't tell you."

"I'm sure of that," he sneered. "It is knowledge a man keeps to himself, isn't it? But, by Heaven, you shall tell me before you leave this place, or--"

"We have already one good ground of quarrel," I interrupted. "What need is there of another?"

"A good ground of quarrel?" he repeated, in a questioning tone.

Honestly I believe that he had for the moment forgotten. His passion for Marie Delhasse and fury at the loss of her filled his whole mind.

"Oh, yes," he went on. "About the duchess? True, Mr. Aycon. That will serve--as well as the truth."

"If that is not a real ground, I know none," said I.

"Haven't you told me that you kept her from me?"

"For no purposes of my own."

He drew back a step, smiling scornfully.

"A man is bound to protest that the lady is virtuous," said he; "but need he insist so much on his own virtue?"

"As it so happens," I observed, "it's not a question of virtue."

I suppose there was something in my tone that caught his attention, for his scornful air was superseded by an intent puzzled gaze, and his next question was put in lower tones:

"What did you stay in Avranches for?"

"Because your wife asked me," said I. The answer was true enough, but, as I wished to deal candidly with him, I added: "And, later on, Mlle. Delhasse expressed a similar desire."

"My wife and Mlle. Delhasse! Truly you are a favorite!"

"Honest men happen to be scarce in this neighborhood," said I. I was becoming rather angry.

"If you are one, I hope to be able to make them scarcer by one more," said the duke.

"Well, we needn't wrangle over it any more," said I; and I sat down on the lid of a chest that stood by the hearth. But the duke sprang forward and seized me by the arm, crying again in ungovernable rage:

"Where is she?"

"She is safe from you, I hope."

"Aye--and you'll keep her safe!"

"As I say, I know nothing about her, except that she'd be an honest girl if you'd let her alone."

He was still holding my arm, and I let him hold it: the man was hardly himself under the slavery of his passion. But again, at my words, the wonder which I had seen before stole into his eyes.

"You must know where she is," he said, with a straining look at my face, "but--but--"

He broke off, leaving his sentence unfinished. Then he broke out again:

"Safe from me? I would make life a heaven for her!"

"That's the old plea," said I.

"Is a thing a lie because it's old? There's nothing in the world I would not give her--nothing I have not offered her." Then he looked at me, repeating again: "You must know where she is." And then he whispered: "Why aren't you with her?"

"I have no wish to be with her," said I. Any other reason would not have appealed to him.

He sank down on the stool again and sat in a heap, breathing heavily and quickly. He was wonderfully transfigured, and I hardly knew in him the cold harsh man who had been my temporary master and was the mocking husband of the duchess. Say all that may be said about his passion, I could not doubt that it was life and death to him. Justification he had none; excuse I found in my heart for him, for it struck me--coming over me in a strange sudden revelation as I sat and looked at him--that he had given such love to the duchess, the gay little lady would have been marvelously embarrassed. It was hers to dwell in a radiant mid-ether, neither to mount to heaver nor descend to hell. And in one of theses two must dwell such feelings as the dukes's.

He roused himself, and leaning forward spoke to me again:

"You've lived in the same house with her and talked to her. You swear you don't love her? What? Has Elsa's little figure come between?"

His tone was full of scorn. He seemed angry with me, not for presuming to love his wife (nay, he would not believe that), but for being so blind as not to love Marie.

"I didn't love her!" I answered, with a frown on my face and slow words.

"You have never felt attracted to her?"

I did not answer that question. I sat frowning in silence till the duke spoke again, in a low hoarse whisper:

"And she? What says she to you?"

I looked up with a start, and met his searching wrathful gaze. I shook my head; his question was new to me--new and disturbing.

"I don't know," said I; and on that we sat in silence for many moments.

Then he rose abruptly and stood beside me.

"Mr. Aycon," he said, in the smoother tones in which he had begun our curious interview, "I came near a little while ago to doing a ruffianly thing, of a sort I am not wont to do. We must fight out our quarrel in the proper way. Have you any friends in the neighborhood?"

"I am quite unknown," I answered.

He thought for an instant, and then continued:

"There is a regiment quartered at Pontorson, and I have acquaintances among the officers. If agreeable to you, we will drive over there; we shall find gentlemen ready to assist us."

"You are determined to fight?" I asked.

"Yes," he said, with a snap of his lips. "Have we not matters enough and to spare to fight about?"

"I can't of course deny that you have a pretext."

"And I, Mr. Aycon, know that I have also a cause. Will this morning suit you?”

"It is hard on two now."

"Precisely. We have time for a little rest; then I will order the carriage and we will drive together to Pontorson."

"You mean that I should stay in your house?"

"If you will so far honor me. I wish to settle this affair at once, so as to be moving."

"I can but accept."

"Indeed you could hardly get back to Avranches, if, as I presume, you came on foot. Ah! you've never told me why you wished to see Jean;" and he turned a questioning look on me again, as he walked toward the door of the cottage.

"It was--" I began.

"Stay; you shall tell me in the house. Shall I lead the way? Ah, but you know it!" and he smiled grimly.

With a bow, I preceded him along the little path where I had once waited for the duchess, and where Pierre, the new servant, had found me. No words passed between us as we went. The duke advanced to the door and unlocked it. We went in, nobody was about, and we crossed the dimly lighted hall into the small room where supper had been laid for three (three who should have been four) on the night of my arrival. Meat, bread, and wine stood on the table now, and with a polite gesture the duke invited me to a repast. I was tired and hungry, and I took a hunch of bread and poured out some wine.

"What keeps Jean, I wonder?" mused the duke, as he sat down. "Perhaps he has found her!" and a gleam of eager hope flashed from his eyes.

I made no comment--where was the profit in more sparring of words? I munched my bread and drank my wine, thinking, by a whimsical turn of thought, of Gustave de Berensac and his horror at the table laid for three. Soon I laid down my napkin, and the duke held out his cigarette case toward me:

"And now, Mr. Aycon, if I'm not keeping you up--"

"I do not feel sleepy," said I.

"It is the same for both of us," he reminded me, shrugging his shoulders. "Well, then, if you are willing--of course you can refuse if you choose--I should like to hear what brought you to Jean's quarters on foot from Avranches in the middle of the night."

"You shall hear. I did not desire to meet you, if I could avoid it, and therefore I sought old Jean, with the intention of making him a messenger to you."

"For what purpose?"

"To restore to you something which has been left on my hands and to which you have a better right than I."

"Pray, what is that?" he asked, evidently puzzled. The truth never crossed his mind.

"This," said I; and I took the red leathern box out of my pocket, and set it down on the table in front of the duke. And I put my cigarette between my lips and leaned back in my chair.

CHAPTER XIII.
A Timely Truce.

I think that at first the Duke of Saint-Maclou could not, as the old saying goes, believe his eyes. He sat looking from me to the red box, and from the red box back to my face. Then he stretched out a slow, wavering hand and drew the box nearer to him till it rested in the circle of his spread-out arm and directly under his poring gaze. He seemed to shrink from opening it; but at last he pressed the spring with a covert timid movement of his finger, and the lid, springing open, revealed the Cardinal's Necklace.

It seemed to be more brilliant than I had ever seen it, in the light of the lamp that stood on the table by us; and the duke looked at it as a magician might at the amulet which had failed him, or a warrior at the talisman that had proved impotent. And I, moved to a sudden anger with him for tempting the girl with such a bribe, said bitterly and scornfully, with fresh indignation rising in me:

"It was a high bid! Strange that you could not buy her with it!"

He paid no visible heed to my taunt; and his tone was dull, bewildered, and heavy as, holding the box still in his curved arm, he asked slowly:

"Did she give it to you to give to me?"

"She gave it to me to give to your wife." He looked up with a start. "But your wife would not take it of her. And when I returned from my errand she was gone--where I know not. So I decided to send it back to you."

He did not follow, or took very little interest in my brief history. He did not even reiterate his belief that I knew Marie's whereabouts. His mind was fixed on another point.

"How did you know she had it?" he asked.

"I found her with it on the table before her--"

"You found her?"

"Yes; I went into her sitting room and found her as I say; and she was sobbing; and I got from her the story of it."

"She told you that?"

"Yes; and she feared to send it back, lest you should come and overbear her resistance. I supposed you had frightened her. But neither would she keep it--"

"You bade her not," he put in, in a quick low tone.

"If you like, I prayed her not. Did it need much cleverness to see what was meant by keeping it?"

His mouth twitched. I saw the tempest rising again in him. But for a little longer he held it down.

"Do you take me for a fool?" he asked.

"Am I a boy--do I know nothing of women? And do I know nothing of men?"

And he ended in a miserable laugh, and then fell again to tugging his mustache with his shaking hand.

"You know," said I, "what's bad in both; and no doubt that's a good deal."

In that very room the duchess had called Gustave de Berensac a preacher. Her husband had much the same reproach for me.

"Sermons are fine from your mouth," he muttered.

And then his self-control gave way. With a sweep of his arm he drove the necklace from him, so that the box whizzed across the table, balanced a moment on the edge, and fell crashing on the ground, while the duke cried:

"God's curse on it and you! You've taken her from me!"

There was danger--there was something like madness--in his aspect as he rose, and, facing me where I sat, went on in tones still low, but charged with a rage that twisted his features and lined his white cheeks:

"Are you a liar or a fool? Have you taken the game for yourself, or are you fool enough not to see that she has despised me--and that miserable necklace--for you--because you've caught her fancy? My God! and I've given my life to it for two years past! And you step in. Why didn't you keep to my wife? You were welcome to her--though I'd have shot you all the same for my name's sake. You must have Marie too, must you?"

He was mad, if ever man was mad, at that moment. But his words were strong with the force and clear with the insight of his passion; and the rush of them carried my mind along, and swept it with them to their own conclusion. Nay, I will not say that--for I doubted still; but I doubted as a man who would deny, not as one who laughs away, a thought. I sat silent, looking, not at him, but at the Cardinal's Necklace on the floor.

Then, suddenly, while I was still busy with the thought and dazzled at the revelation, while I sat bemused, before I could move, his fingers were on my throat, and his face within a foot of mine, glaring and working as he sent his strength into his arms to throttle me. For his wife--and his name--he would fight a duel: for the sake of Marie Delhasse he would do murder on an invited stranger in his house. I struggled to my feet, his grip on my throat; and I stretched out my hands and caught him under the shoulders in the armpits, and flung him back against the table, and thence he reeled on to a large cabinet that was by the wall, and Stood leaning against it.

"I knew you were a villain," I said, "but I thought you were a gentleman." (I did not stop to consider the theory implied in that.)

He leaned against the cabinet, red with his exertion and panting; but he did not come at me again. He dashed his hand across his forehead and then he said in hoarse breathless tones:

"You shan't leave here alive!"

Then, with a start of recollection, he thrust his hand into his pocket and brought out a key. He put it in the lock of a drawer of the cabinet, fumbling after the aperture and missing it more than once. Then he opened the drawer, took out a pair of dueling pistols, and laid them on the table.

"They're loaded," he said. "Examine them for yourself."

I did not move; but I took my little friend out of my pocket.

"If I'm attacked," said I, "I shall defend myself; but I'm not going to fight a duel here, without witnesses, at the dead of night, in your house."

"Call it what you like then," said he; and he snatched up a pistol from the table.

He was beyond remonstrance, influence, or control. I believe that in a moment he would have fired; and I must have fired also, or gone to my death as a sheep to the slaughter. But as he spoke there came a sound, just audible, which made him pause, with his right hand that held the pistol raised halfway to the level of his shoulder.

Faint as the sound was, slight as the interruption it would seem to offer to the full career of a madman's fury, it was yet enough to check him, to call him back to consciousness of something else in the world than his balked passion and the man whom he deemed to have thwarted it.

"What's that?" he whispered.

It was the lowest, softest knock at the door--a knock that even in asking attention almost shrank from being heard. It was repeated, louder, yet hardly audibly. The duke, striding on the tip of his toes, transferred the pistols from the table back to the drawer, and stood with his hand inside the open drawer: I slid my weapon into my pocket; and then he trod softly across the floor to the door.

"One moment!" I whispered.

And I stooped and picked up the Cardinal's Necklace and put it back where it had lain before, pushing its box under the table by a hasty movement of my foot--for the duke, after a nod of intelligence, was already opening the door. I drew back in the shadow behind it and waited.

"What do you want?" asked the duke.

And then a girl stepped hastily into the room and closed the door quickly and noiselessly behind her. I saw her face: she was my old friend Suzanne. When her eyes fell on me, she started in surprise, as well she might; but the caution and fear, which had made her knock almost noiseless, her tread silent, and her face all astrain with alert alarm, held her back from any cry.

"Never mind him," said the duke. "That's nothing to do with you. What do you want?"

"Hush! Speak low. I thought you would still be up, as you told me to refill the lamp and have it burning. There's--there's something going on."

She spoke in a quick, urgent whisper, and in her agitation remembered no deference in her words of address. "Going on? Where? Do you mean here?"

"No, no! I heard nothing here. In the duchess's dressing-room: it is just under the room where I sleep. I awoke about half an hour ago, and I heard sounds from there. There was a sound as of muffled hammering, and then a noise, like the rasping of a file; and I thought I heard people moving about, but very cautiously."

The duke and I were both listening attentively.

"I was frightened, and lay still a little; but then I got up--for the sounds went on--and put on some clothes, and came down--"

"Why didn't you rouse the men? It must be thieves."

"I did go to the men's room; but their door was locked, and I could not make them hear. I did not dare to knock loud; but I saw a light in the room, under the door; and if they'd been awake they would have heard."

"Perhaps they weren't there," I suggested.

Suzanne turned a sudden look on me. Then she said:

"The safe holding the jewels is fixed in the wall of the duchess' dressing room. And--and Lafleur knows it."

The duke had heard the story with a frowning face; but now a smile appeared on his lips, and he said:

"Ah, yes! The jewels are there!"

"The--the Cardinal's Necklace," whispered Suzanne.

"True," said the duke; and his eyes met mine, and we both smiled. A few minutes ago it had not seemed likely that I should share a joke--even a rather grim joke--with him.

"Mr. Aycon," said he, "are you inclined to help me to look into this matter? It may be only the girl's fancy--"

"No, no; I heard plainly," Suzanne protested eagerly.

"But one can never trust these rascally men-servants."

"I am quite ready," said I.

"Our business," said he, "will wait."

"It will be the better for waiting."

He hesitated a moment; then he assented gravely:

"You're right--much better."

He took a pistol out of the drawer, and shut and locked the drawer. Then he turned to Suzanne and said:

"You had better go back to bed."

"I daren't, I daren't!"

"Then stay here and keep quiet. Mind, not a sound!"

"Give me a pistol."

He unlocked the drawer again, and gave her what she asked. Then signing to me to follow him, he opened the door, and we stepped together into the dark hall, the duke laying his hand on my arm and whispering:

"They're after the necklace."

We groped slowly, with careful noiselessness, across the hall to the foot of the great staircase. There we paused and listened. There was nothing to be heard. We climbed the first flight of stairs, and the duke turned sharp to the right. We were now in a short corridor which ran north and south; three yards ahead of us was another turn, leading to the west wing of the house. There was a window by us; the duke gently opened it; and over against us, across the base of the triangle formed by the building, was another window, four or five yards away. The window was heavily curtained; no light could be seen through it. But as we stood listening, the sounds began--first the gentle muffled hammering, then the sound of the file. The duke still held my arm, and we stood motionless. The sounds went on for a while. Then they ceased. There was a pause of complete stillness. Then a sharp, though not loud, click! And, upon this, the duke whispered to me:

"They've got the safe open. Now they'll find the small portable safe which holds the necklace."

And I could make out an amused smile on his pale face. Before I could speak, he turned and began to crawl away. I followed. We descended the stairs again to the hall. At the foot he turned sharply to the left, and came to a standstill in a recess under the staircase.

"We'll wait here. Is your pistol all right?"

"Yes, all right," said I.

And, as I spoke, the faintest sound spread from the top of the stairs, and a board creaked under the steps of a man. I was close against the duke, and I felt him quiver with a stifled laugh. Meanwhile the Cardinal's Necklace pressed hard against my ribs under my tightly buttoned coat.

CHAPTER XIV.
For an Empty Box.

When I look back on the series of events which I am narrating and try to recover the feelings with which I was affected in its passage, I am almost amazed and in some measure ashamed to find how faint is my abhorrence of the Duke of Saint-Maclou. My indignation wants not the bridle but the whip, and I have to spur myself on to a becoming vehemence of disapproval. I attribute my sneaking kindness for him--for to that and not much less I must plead guilty--partly indeed to the revelation of a passion in him that seemed to leave him hardly responsible for the wrong he plotted, but far more to the incidents of this night, in which I was in a manner his comrade and the partner with him in an adventure. To have stood shoulder to shoulder with a man blinds his faults--and the duke bore himself, not merely with the coolness and courage which I made no doubt of his displaying, but with a readiness and zest remarkable at any time, but more striking when they followed on the paroxysm to which I had seen him helplessly subject. These indications of good in the man mollified my dislike and attached me to him by a bond which begot toleration and resists even the clearer and more piercing analysis of memory. Therefore, when those who speak to me of what he did and sought to do say what I cannot help admitting to be true, I hold my peace, thinking that the duke and I have played as partners as well as on hostile sides, and that I, being no saint, may well hold my tongue about the faults of a fellow-sinner. Moreover,--and this is the thing of all strongest to temper or to twist my judgment of him,--I feel often as though it were he who laid his finger on my blind eyes and bade me look up and see where lay my happiness. For it is strange how long a man can go without discovering his own undermost desire. Yet, when seen, how swift it grows!

Quiet and still we stood in the bay of the staircase, and the steps over our heads creaked under the feet of the men who came down. The duke's hand was on my arm, restraining me, and he held it there till the feet had passed above us and the stealthy tread landed on the marble flagging of the hall. We thrust our heads out and peered through the darkness. I saw the figures of two men, one following the other toward the front door; this the first and taller unfastened and noiselessly opened; and he and his fellow, whom, by the added light which entered, I perceived to be carrying a box or case of moderate size, waited for a moment on the threshold. Then they passed out, drawing the door close after them.

Still the duke held me back, and we rested where we were three or four minutes. Then he whispered, "Come," and we stole across the hall after them and found ourselves outside. It must have been about half-past two o'clock in the morning; there was no moon and it was rather dark. The duke turned sharp to the left and led me to the bypath, and there, a couple of hundred yards ahead of us, we saw a cube of light that came from a dark lantern.

The duke's face was dimly visible, and an amused smile played on his lips as he said softly:

"Lafleur and Pierre! They think they've got the necklace!"

Was this the meaning of Pierre's appearance in the role of my successor? The idea suggested itself to me in a moment, and I strove to read my companion's face for a confirmation.

"We'll see where they go," he whispered, and then laid his finger on his lips. Amusement sounded in his voice; indeed it was impossible not to perceive the humor of the position, when I felt the Cardinal's Necklace against my own ribs.

We were walking now under cover of the trees which lined the sides of the path, so that no backward glance could discover us to the thieves; and I was wondering how long we were thus to dog their steps, when suddenly they turned to the left about fifty yards short of the spot where old Jean's cottage stood, and disappeared from our sight. We emerged into the path, the duke taking the lead. He was walking more briskly now, and I saw him examine his pistol. When we came where the fellows had turned, we followed in their track.

The first distant hint of approaching morning caught the tops of the trees above us, turning them from black to a deep chill gray, as we paused to listen. Our pursuit had brought us directly behind the cottage, which now stood about a hundred yards on the right; and then we came upon them--or rather suddenly stopped and crouched down to avoid coming upon them--where they were squatting on the ground with a black iron box between them, and the lantern's light thrown on the keyhole of the box. Lafleur held the lantern; Pierre's hand was near the lock, and I presumed--I could not see--that he held some instrument with which he meant to open it. A ring of trees framed the picture, and the men sat in a hollow, well hidden from the path even had it been high day.

The Duke of Saint-Maclou touched my arm, and I leaned forward to look in his face. He nodded, and, brushing aside the trees, we sprang out upon the astonished fellows. Fora moment they did not move, struck motionless with surprise, while we stood over them, pistols in hand. We had caught them fair and square. Expecting no interruption, they had guarded against none. Their weapons were in their pockets, their hands busy with their job. They sprang up the next moment; but the duke's muzzle covered Lafleur, and mine was leveled full at Pierre. A second later Lafleur fell on his knees with a cry for mercy; the little man stood quite still, his arms by his side and the iron box hard by his feet. Lafleur's protestations and lamentations began to flow fast. Pierre shrugged his shoulders. The duke advanced, and I kept pace with him.

"Keep your eye on that fellow, Mr. Aycon," said the duke; and then he put his left hand in his pocket, took out a key and flung it in Lafleur's face. It struck him sharply between the eyes, and he whined again.

"Open the box," said the duke. "Open it--do you hear? This instant!"

With shaking hands the fellow dragged the box from where it lay by Pierre's feet, and dropping on his knees began to fumble with the lock. At last he contrived to unlock it, and raised the lid. The duke sprang forward and, catching him by the nape of the neck, crammed his head down into the box, bidding him, "Look--look--look!" And while he said it he laughed, and took advantage of Lafleur's posture to give him four or five hearty kicks.

"It's empty!" cried Lafleur, surprise rescuing him for an instant from the other emotions to which his position gave occasion. And, as he spoke, for the first time Pierre started, turning an eager gaze toward the box.

"Yes, it's empty," said the duke. "The necklace isn't there, is it? Now, tell me all about it, or I'll put a bullet through your head!"

Then the story came: disentangled from the excuses and prayers, it was simply that Pierre was no footman but a noted thief--that he had long meditated an attack on the Cardinal's Necklace; had made Lafleur's acquaintance in Paris, corrupted his facile virtue, and, with the aid of forged testimonials, presented himself in the character in which I had first made his acquaintance. The rascals had counted on the duke's preoccupation with Marie Delhasse for their opportunity. The duke smiled to hear it. Pierre listened to the whole story without a word of protest or denial; his accomplice's cowardly attempt to present him as the only culprit gained no more notice than another shrug and a softly muttered oath. "Destiny," the little man seemed to say in the eloquent movement of his shoulders; while the growing light showed his beady eyes fixed, full and unfaltering, on me.

Lafleur's prayers died away. The duke, still smiling, set his pistol against the wretch's head.

"That's what you deserve," said he.

And Lafleur, groveling, caught him by the knees.

"Don't kill me! Don't kill me!" he implored.

"Why not?" asked the duke, in the tone of a man willing to hear the other side, but certain that he would not be convinced by it. "Why not? We find you stealing--and we shoot you as you try to escape. I see nothing unnatural or illegal in it, Lafleur. Nor do I see anything in favor of leaving you alive."

And the pistol pressed still on Lafleur's forehead. Whether his master meant to shoot, I know not--although I believe he did. But Lafleur had little doubt of his purpose; for he hastened to play his best card, and, clinging still to the duke's knees, cried desperately:

"If you'll spare me, I'll tell you where she is!"

The duke's arm fell to his side; and in a changed voice, from which the cruel bantering had fled, while eager excitement filled its place, he cried:

"What? Where who is?"

"The lady--Mlle. Delhasse. A girl I know--there in Avranches--saw her go. She is there now."

"Where, man, where?" roared the duke, stamping his foot, and menacing the wretch again with his pistol.

I turned to listen, forgetful of quiet little Pierre and his alert beady eyes; yet I kept the pistol on him.

And Lafleur cried:

"At the convent--at the convent, on the shores of the bay!"

"My God!" cried the duke, and his eyes suddenly turned and flashed on mine; and I saw that the necklace was forgotten, that our partnership was ended, and that I again, and no longer the cowering creature before him, was the enemy. And I also, hearing that Marie Delhasse was at the convent, was telling myself that I was a fool not to have thought of it before, and wondering what new impulse had seized the duke's wayward mind.

Thus neither the duke nor I was attending to the business of the moment. But there was a man of busy brain, whose life taught him to profit by the slips of other men and to let pass no opportunities. Our carelessness gave one now--a chance of escape, and a chance of something else too. For, while my negligent hand dropped to my side and my eyes were seeking to read the duke's face, the figure opposite me must have been moving. Softly must a deft hand have crept to a pocket; softly came forth the hidden weapon. There was a report loud and sudden; and then another. And with the first, Lafleur, who was kneeling at the duke's feet and looking up to see how his shaft had sped, flung his arms wildly over his head, gave a shriek, and fell dead--his head, half-shattered, striking the iron box as he fell sideways in a heap on the ground.

The duke sprang back with an oath, whose sound was engulfed in the second discharge of Pierre's pistol: and I felt myself struck in the right arm; and my weapon fell to the ground, while I clutched the wounded limb with my left hand.

The duke, after a moment's hesitation and bewilderment, raised his pistol and fired; but the active little scoundrel was safe among the trees, and we heard the twigs cracking and the leaves rustling as he pushed his way through the wood. He was gone--scot free for us, but with his score to Lafleur well paid. I swayed where I stood, to and fro: the pain was considerable, and things seemed to go round before my eyes; yet I turned to my companion, crying:

"After him! He'll get off! I'm hit; I can't run!"

The duke stood still, frowning; then he slowly dropped his smoking pistol into his pocket. For a moment longer he stood, and a smile broadened on his face as he raised his eyes to me.

"Let him," he said briefly; and his glance rested on me for a moment in defiant significance. And then, without another word, he turned on his heel. He took no heed of Lafleur's dead body, that seemed to fondle the box, huddling it in a ghastly embrace, nor of me, who swayed and tottered and sank on the ground by the corpse. With set lips and eager eyes he passed me, taking the road by which we had come. And I, hugging my wounded arm, with open eyes and parted lips, saw him dive in among the trees and disappear toward the house. And I looked round on the iron box and the dead body--two caskets robbed of all that made them more than empty lumber.

Minute followed minute; and then I heard the hoofs of a horse galloping at full speed along the road from the house toward Avranches. Lafleur was dead and done with; Pierre might go his ways; I lay fainting in the wood; the Cardinal's Necklace was still against my side. What recked the Duke of Saint-Maclou of all that? I knew, as I heard the thud of the hoofs on the road, that by the time the first reddening rays reached over the horizon he would be at the convent, seeking the woman who was all the world to him.

And I sat there helpless, fearful of what would befall her. For what could a convent full of women avail against his mastering rage? And a sudden sharp pang ran through me, startling even myself in its intensity; so that I cried out aloud, raising my sound arm in the air toward Heaven, like a man who swears a vow:

"By God, no! By God, no--no!"

CHAPTER XV.
I Choose my Way.

The dead man lay there, embracing the empty box that had brought him to his death; and for many minutes I sat within a yard of him, detained by the fascination and grim mockery of the picture no less than by physical weakness and a numbness of my brain. My body refused to act, and my mind hardly urged its indolent servant. I was in sore distress for Marie Delhasse,-- my vehement cry witnessed it,--yet I had not the will to move to her aid; will and power both seemed to fail me. I could fear, I could shrink with horror, but I could not act; nor did I move till the increasing pain of my wound drove me, as it might any unintelligent creature, to scramble to my feet and seek, half-blindly, for some place that should afford shelter and succor.

Leaving Lafleur and the box where they lay, a pretty spectacle for a moralist, I stumbled through the wood back to the path, and stood there in helpless vacillation. At the house I should find better attendance, but old Jean's cottage was nearer. The indolence of weakness gained the day, and I directed my steps toward the cottage, thinking now, so far as I can recollect, of none of the exciting events of the night nor even of what the future still held, but purely and wholly of the fact that in the cottage I should find a fire and a bed. The root-instincts of the natural man--the primeval elementary wants--asserted their supremacy and claimed a monopoly of my mind, driving out all rival emotions, and with a mighty sigh of relief and content I pushed open the door of the cottage, staggered across to the fire and sank down on the stool by it, thanking Heaven for so much, and telling myself that soon, very soon, I should feel strong enough to make my way into the inner room and haul out Jean's pallet and set it by the fire and stretch my weary limbs, and, if the pain of my wound allowed me, go to sleep. Beyond that my desires did not reach, and I forgot all my fears save the one dread that I was too weak for the desired effort. Certainly it is hard for a man to think himself a hero!

I took no note of time, but I must have sat where I was for many minutes, before I heard someone moving in the inner room. I was very glad; of course it was Jean, and Jean, I told myself with luxurious self-congratulation, would bring the bed for me, and put something on my wound, and maybe give me a chink of some fine hot cognac that would spread life through my veins. Thus I should be comfortable and able to sleep, and forget all the shadowy people--they seemed but shadows half-real--that I had been troubling my brain about: the duke, and Marie, whose face danced for a moment before my eyes, and that dead fellow who hugged the box so ludicrously. So I tried to call to Jean, but the trouble was too great, and, as he would be sure to come out soon, I waited; and I blinked at the smoldering wood-ashes in the fire till my eyes closed and the sleep was all but come, despite the smart of my arm and the ache in my unsupported back.

But just before I had forgotten everything the door of the inner room creaked and opened. My side was toward it and I did not look round. I opened my eyes and feebly waved my left hand. Then a voice came, clear and fresh:

"Jean, is it you? Well, is the duke at the house?"

I must be dreaming; that was my immediate conviction, for the voice that I heard was a voice I knew well, but one not likely to be heard here, in Jean's cottage, at four o'clock in the morning. Decidedly I was dreaming, and as in order to dream a man must be asleep, I was pleased at the idea and nodded happily, smiling and blinking in self-congratulation. But that pleasant minute of illusion was my last; for the voice cried in tones too full of animation, too void of dreamy vagueness, too real and actual to let me longer set them down as made of my own brain:

"Heaven! Why, it's Mr. Aycon! How in the world do you come here?"

To feel surprise at the Duchess of Saint-Maclou doing anything which she might please to do or being anywhere that the laws of Nature rendered it possible she should be, was perhaps a disposition of mind of which I should have been by this time cured; yet I was surprised to find her standing in the doorway that led from Jean's little bedroom dressed in a neat walking gown and a very smart hat, her hands clasped in the surprise which she shared with me and her eyes gleaming with an amused delight which found, I fear, no answer in my heavy bewildered gaze.

"I'm getting warm," said I at first, but then I made an effort to rouse myself. "I was a bit hurt, you know," I went on; "that little villain Pierre--"

"Hurt!" cried the duchess, springing forward. "How? Oh, my dear Mr. Aycon, how pale you are!"

After that remark of the duchess', I remember nothing which occurred for a long while. In fact, just as I had apprehended that I was awake, that the duchess was real, and that it was most remarkable to find her in Jean's cottage, I fainted, and the duchess, the cottage, and everything else vanished from sight and mind.

When next I became part of the waking world I found myself on the sofa of the little room in the duke's house which I was beginning to know so well. I felt very comfortable: my arm was neatly bandaged, I wore a clean shirt. Suzanne was spreading a meal on the table, and the duchess, in a charming morning gown, was smiling at me and humming a tune. The clock on the mantelpiece marked a quarter to eight.

"Now I know all about it," said the duchess, perceiving my revival. "I've heard it all from Suzanne and Jean--or anyhow I can guess the rest. And you mustn't tire yourself by talking. I had you brought here so that you might be well looked after; because we're so much indebted to you, you know."

"Is the duke here?" I asked.

"Oh, dear, no; it's all right," nodded the duchess. "I don't know--and I do not care--where the duke is. Drink this milk, Mr. Aycon. Your arm's not very bad, you know--Jean says it isn't, I mean--but you'd better have milk first, and something to eat when you feel stronger."

The duchess appeared to be in excellent spirits. She caught up a bit of toast from the table, poured out a cup of coffee, and, still moving about, began a light breakfast, with every sign of appetite and enjoyment.

"You've come back?" said I, looking at her in persistent surprise.

Suzanne put the cushions behind my back in a more comfortable position, smiled kindly on us, and left us.

"Yes," said the duchess, "I have for the present, Mr. Aycon."

"But--but the duke--" I stammered.

"I don't mind the duke," said she. "Besides, he may not come. It's rather nice that you're just a little hurt. Don't you think so, Mr. Aycon? Just a little, you know."

"Why?" was all I found to say. The reason was not clear to me.

"Why, in the first place, because you can't fight till your arm's well--oh, yes, of course Armand was going to fight you--and, in the second place, you can and must stay here. There's no harm in it, while you're ill, you see; Armand can't say there is. It's rather funny, isn't it, Mr. Aycon?" and she munched a morsel of toast, and leaned her elbows on the table and sent a sparkling glance across at me, for all the world as she had done on the first night I knew her. The cares of the world did not gall the shoulders of Mme. de Saint-Maclou.

"But why are you here?" said I, sticking to my point.

The duchess set down the cup of coffee which she had been sipping.

"I am not particular," said she. "But I told the Mother Superior exactly what I told the duke. She wouldn't listen any more than he would. However, I was resolved; so I came here. I don't see where else I could go, do you, Mr. Aycon?"

"What did you tell the Mother?"

The duchess stretched one hand across the table, clenching her small fist and tapping gently with it on the cloth.

"There is one thing that I will not do, Mr. Aycon," said she, a touch of red coming in her cheeks and her lips set in obstinate lines. "I don't care whether the house is my house or anybody else's house, or an inn--yes, or a convent either. But I will not be under the same roof with Marie Delhasse."

And her declaration finished, the duchess nodded most emphatically, and turned to her cup again.

The name of Marie Delhasse, shot forth from Mme. de Saint-Maclou's pouting lips, pierced the cloud that had seemed to envelop my brain. I sat up on the sofa and looked eagerly at the duchess.

"You saw her, then, at the convent?" I asked.

"Yes, I met her in the chapel. Really, I should have expected to be safe from her there. And the Mother would not turn her out!" And then the duchess, by a sudden transition, said to me, with a half-apologetic, half challenging smile: "You got my note, I suppose, Mr. Aycon?"

For a minute I regarded the duchess. And I smiled, and my smile turned to a laugh as I answered:

"Oh, yes! I got the note."

"I meant it," said she. "But I suppose I must forgive you now. You've been so brave, and you're so much hurt." And the duchess' eyes expressed a gratifying admiration of my powers.

I fingered my arm, which lay comfortably enough in the bandages and the sling that Suzanne's care had provided for it. And I rose to my feet.

"Oh, you mustn't move!" cried the duchess, rising also and coming to where I stood.

"By Jove, but I must!" said I, looking at the clock. "The duke's got four hours' start of me."

"What do you want with my husband now?" she asked. "I don't see why you should fight him; anyhow, you can't fight him till your arm is well."

The duchess' words struck on my ear and her dainty little figure was before my eyes, but my thoughts were absent from her.

"Don't go, Mr. Aycon," said she.

"I must go," I said. "By this time he'll be at the convent."

A frown gathered on the duchess' face.

"What concern is it of yours?" she asked. "I--I mean, what good can you do?"

"I can hardly talk to you about it--" I began awkwardly; but the duchess saved me the trouble of finishing my sentence, for she broke in angrily:

"Oh, as if I believe that! Mr. Aycon, why are you going?"

"I'm going to see that the duke doesn't--"

"Oh, you are very anxious--and very good, aren't you? Yes, and very chivalrous! Mr. Aycon, I don't care what he does;" and she looked at me defiantly.

"But I do," said I, and seeing my hat on the cabinet by the wall, I walked across the room and stretched out my hand for it. The duchess darted after me and stood between my hat and me.

"Why do you care?" she asked, with a stamp of her small foot.

There were, no doubt, many most sound and plausible reasons for caring--reasons independent of any private feelings of my own in regard to Marie Delhasse; but not one of them did I give to the duchess. I stood before her, looking, I fear, very embarrassed, and avoiding her accusing eyes.

Then the duchess flung her head back, and with passionate scorn said to me:

"I believe you're in love with the woman yourself!"

And to this accusation also I made no reply.

"Are you really going?" she asked, her voice suddenly passing to a note of entreaty.

"I must go," said I obstinately, callously, curtly.

"Then go!" cried the duchess. "And never let me see you again!"

She moved aside, and I sprang forward and seized my hat. I took no notice of the duchess, and, turning, I walked straight toward the door. But before I reached it the duchess flung herself on the sofa and buried her face in the cushions. I would not leave her like that, so I stood and waited; but my tongue still refused to find excuses, and still I was in a fever to be off.

But the duchess rose again and stood upright. She was rather pale and her lips quivered, but she held out her hand to me with a smile. And suddenly I understood what I was doing, and that for the second time the proud little lady before me saw herself left and neglected for the sake of that woman whose presence made even a convent uninhabitable to her; and the bitter wound that her pride suffered was declared in her bearing and in the pathetic effort at dignity which she had summoned up to hide her pain. Yet, although on this account I was sorry for her, I discerned nothing beyond hurt pride, and was angry at the pride for the sake of Marie Delhasse, and when I spoke it was in defense of Marie Delhasse, and not in comfort to the duchess.

"She is not what you think," I said.

The duchess drew herself up to her full height, making the most of her inches.

"Really, Mr. Aycon," said she, "you must forgive me if I do not discuss that." And she paused, and then added, with a curl of her lip: "You and my husband can settle that between you;" and with a motion of her hand she signed to me to leave her.

Looking back on the matter, I do not know that I had any reason to be ashamed or to feel myself in any sort a traitor to the duchess. Yet some such feelings I had as I backed out of the room leaving her standing there in unwonted immobility, her eyes haughty and cold, her lips set, her grace congealed to stateliness, her gay agility frozen to proud stiffness.

And I left her thus standing in obedience to the potent yet still but half-understood spell which drew me from her side and would not suffer me to rest, while the Duke of Saint-Maclou was working his devices in the valley beneath the town of Avranches.

CHAPTER XVI.
The Inn near Pontorson.

The moment I found myself outside the house--and I must confess that, for reasons which I have indicated, it was a relief to me to find myself there--I hastened to old Jean's cottage. The old man was eating his breakfast; his stolidity was unshaken by the events of the night; he manifested nothing beyond a mild satisfaction that the two rascals had justified his opinion of them, and a resigned regret that Pierre had not shared the fate of Lafleur. He told me that his inquiries after Marie Delhasse had been fruitless, and added that he supposed there would be a police inquiry into the attempted robbery and the consequent death of Lafleur; indeed he was of opinion that the duke had gone to Avranches to arrange for it as much as to prosecute his search for Marie. I seized the opportunity to suggest that I should be a material witness, and urged him to give me one of the duke's horses to carry me to Avranches. He grumbled at my request, declaring that I should end by getting him into trouble; but a few francs overcame his scruples, and he provided me with a sturdy animal, which I promised to bring or send back in the course of the day.

Great as my impatience was, I was compelled to spend the first hour of my arrival at Avranches under the doctor's hands. He discovered to my satisfaction that the bullet had not lodged in my arm and that my hurt was no more than a flesh-wound, which would, if all went well, heal in a few days. He enjoined perfect rest and freedom from worry and excitement. I thanked him, bowed myself out, mounted again, and rode to the hotel, where I left my horse with instructions for its return to its owner. Then, at my best speed, I hastened down the hill again, reached the grounds of the convent, and approached the door. Perfect rest and freedom from excitement were unattainable until I had learned whether Marie Delhasse was still safe within the old white walls which I saw before me; for, though I could not trace how the change in me had come, nor track its growth, I knew now that if she were there the walls held what was of the greatest moment to me in all the world, and that if she were not there the world was a hell to me until I found her.

I was about to ring the bell, when from the gate of the burial-ground the Mother Superior came at a slow pace. The old woman was frowning as she walked, and her frown deepened at sight of me. But I, caring nothing for what she thought, ran up to her, crying before I had well reached her:

"Is Marie Delhasse still here?"

The Mother stopped dead, and regarded me with disapprobation.

"What business is it of yours, sir, where the young woman is?" she asked.

"I mean her no harm," I urged eagerly. "If she is safe here, I ask to know no more; I don't even ask to see her. Is she here? The Duchess of Saint-Maclou told me that you refused to send her away."

"God forbid that I should send away any sinner who will find refuge here," she said solemnly. "You have seen the duchess?"

"Yes; she is at home. But Mlle. Delhasse?"

But the old woman would not be hurried. She asked again:

"What concern have you, sir, with Marie Delhasse?"

I looked her in the face as I answered plainly:

"To save her from the Duke of Saint-Maclou."

"And from her own mother, sir?"

"Yes, above all from her own mother."

The old woman started at my words; but there was no change in the level calm of her voice as she asked:

"And why would you rescue her?"

"For the same reason that any gentleman would, if he could. If you want more--"

She held up her hand to silence me; but her look was gentler and her voice softer, as she said:

"You, sir, cannot save, and I cannot save, those who will not let God himself save them."

"What do you mean?" I cried in a frenzy of fear and eagerness.

"I had prayed for her, and talked with her. I thought I had seen grace in her. Well, I know not. It is true that she acted as her mother bade her. But I fear all is not well."

"I pray you to speak plainly. Where is she?"

"I do not know where she is. What I know, sir, you shall know, for I believe you come in honesty. This morning--some two hours ago--a carriage drove from the town here. Mme. Delhasse was in it, and with her the Duke of Saint-Maclou. I could not refuse to let the woman see her daughter. They spoke together for a time; and then they called me, and Marie--yes, Marie herself--begged me to let her see the duke. So they came here where we stand, and I stood a few yards off. They talked earnestly in low tones. And at last Marie came to me (the others remaining where they were), and took my hand and kissed it, thanking me and bidding me adieu. I was grieved, sir, for I trusted that the girl had found peace here; and she was in the way to make us love her. 'Does your mother bid you go?' I asked, 'And will she save you from all harm?' And she answered: 'I go of my own will, Mother; but I go hoping to return.' 'You swear that you go of your own will?' I asked. 'Yes, of my own will,' she said firmly; but she was near to weeping as she spoke. Yet what could I do? I could but tell her that our door--God's door--was never shut. That I told her; and with a heavy heart, being able to do nothing else, I let her go. I pray God no harm come of it. But I thought the man's face wore a look of triumph."

"By Heaven," I cried, "it shall not wear it for long! Which way did they go?"

She pointed to the road by the side of the bay, leading away from Avranches.

"That way. I watched the carriage and its dust till I saw it no more, because of the wood that lies between here and the road. You pursue them, sir?"

"To the world's end, madame, if I must."

She sighed and opened her lips to speak, but no words came; and without more, I turned and left her, and set my face to follow the carriage. I was, I think, half-mad with anger and bewilderment, for I did not think that it would be time well spent to ascend to the town and obtain a vehicle or a horse; but I pressed on afoot, weary and in pain as I was, along the hot white road. For now indeed my heart was on fire, and I knew that beside Marie Delhasse everything was nothing. So at first imperceptibly, slowly, and unobserved, but at the last with a swift resistless rush, the power of her beauty and of the soul that I had seemed to see in her won upon me;

and that moment, when I thought that she had yielded to her enemy and mine, was the flowering and bloom of my love for her.

Where had they gone? Not to the duke's house, or I should have met them as I rode down earlier in the morning. Then where? France was wide, and the world wider: my steps were slow. Where lay the use of the chase? In the middle of the road, when I had gone perhaps a mile, I stopped dead. I was beaten and sick at heart, and I searched for a nook of shade by the wayside, and flung myself on the ground; and the ache of my arm was the least of my pain.

As I lay there, my eye caught sight of a cloud of dust on the road. For a moment I scanned it eagerly, and then fell back with a curse of disappointment. It was caused by a man on a horse--and the man was not the duke. But in an instant I was sitting up again--for as the rider drew nearer, trotting briskly along, his form and air was familiar to me; and when he came opposite to me, I sprang up and ran out to meet him, crying out to him:

"Gustave! Gustave!"

It was Gustave de Berensac, my friend. He reined in his horse and greeted me--and he greeted me without surprise, but not without apparent displeasure.

"I thought I should find you here still," said he. "I rode over to seek you. Surely you are not at the duchess'?"

His tone was eloquent of remonstrance.

"I've been staying at the inn."

"At the inn?" he repeated, looking at me curiously. "And is the duchess at home?"

"She's at home now. How come you here?"

"Ah, my friend, and how comes your arm in a sling? Well, you shall have my story first. I expect it will prove shorter. I am staying at Pontorson with a friend who is quartered there."

"But you went to Paris."

Gustave leaned clown to me, and spoke in a low impressive tone:

"Gilbert," said he, "I've had a blow. The day after I got to Paris I heard from Lady Cynthia. She's going to be married to a countryman of yours."

Gustave looked very doleful. I murmured condolence, though in truth I cared, just then, not a straw about the matter.

"So," he continued, "I seized the first opportunity for a little change."

There was a pause. Gustave's mournful eye ranged over the landscape. Then he said, in a patient, sorrowful voice:

"You said the duchess was at home?"

"Yes, she's at home now."

"Ah! I ask again, because as I passed the inn on the way between here and Pontorson I saw in the courtyard--"

"Yes, yes, what?" cried I in sudden eagerness.

"What's the matter, man? I saw a carriage with some luggage on it, and it looked like the duke's, and--Hallo! Gilbert, where are you going?"

"I can't wait, I can't wait!" I called, already three or four yards away.

"But I haven't heard how you got your arm--"

"I can't tell you now. I can't wait!"

My lethargy had vanished; I was hot to be on my way again.

"Is the man mad?" he cried; and he put his horse to a quick walk to keep up with me.

I stopped short.

"It would take all day to tell you the story," I said impatiently.

"Still I should like to know--"

"I can't help it. Look here, Gustave, the duchess knows. Go and see her. I must go on now."

Across the puzzled mournful eyes of the rejected lover and bewildered friend I thought I saw a little gleam.

"The duchess?" said he.

"Yes, she's all alone. The duke's not there."

"Where is the duke?" he asked; but, as it struck me, now rather in precaution than in curiosity.

"That's what I'm going to see," said I.

And with hope and resolution born again in my heart I broke into a fair run, and, with a wave of my hand, left Gustave in the middle of the road, staring after me and plainly convinced that I was mad. Perhaps I was not far from that state. Mad or not, in any case after three minutes I thought no more of my good friend Gustave de Berensac, nor of aught else, save the inn outside Pontorson, just where the old road used to turn toward Mont St. Michel. To that goal I pressed on, forgetting my weariness and my pain. For it might be that the carriage would still stand in the yard, and that in the house I should come upon the object of my search.

Half an hour's walk brought me to the inn, and there, to my joy, I saw the carriage drawn up under a shed side by side with the inn-keeper's market cart. The horses had been taken out; there was no servant in sight. I walked up to the door of the inn and passed through it. And I called for wine.

A big stout man, wearing a blouse, came out to meet me. The inn was a large one, and the inn-keeper was evidently a man of some consideration, although he wore a blouse. But I did not like the look of him, for he had shifty eyes and a bloated face. Without a word he brought me what I ordered and set it down in a little room facing the stable yard.

"Whose carriage is that under your shed?" I asked, sipping my wine.

"It is the carriage of the Duke of Saint-Maclou, sir," he answered readily enough.

"The duke is here, then?"

"Have you business with him, sir?"

"I did but ask you a simple question," said I. "Ah! what's that? Who's that?"

I had been looking out of the window, and my sudden exclamation was caused by this--that the door of a stable which faced me had opened very gently, and but just wide enough to allow a face to appear for an instant and then disappear. And it seemed to me that I knew the face, although the sight of it had been too short to make me sure.

"What did you see, sir?" asked the inn-keeper. (The name on his signboard was Jacques Bontet.)

I turned and faced him full.

"I saw someone look out of the stable," said I.

"Doubtless the stable-boy," he answered; and his manner was so ordinary, unembarrassed, and free from alarm, that I doubted whether my eyes had not played me a trick, or my imagination played one upon my eyes.

Be that as it might, I had no time to press my host further at that moment; for I heard a step behind me and a voice I knew saying:

"Bontet, who is this gentleman?"

I turned. In the doorway of the room stood the Duke of Saint-Maclou. He was in the same dress as when he had parted from me; he was dusty, his face was pale, and the skin had made bags under his eyes. But he stood looking at me composedly, with a smile on his lips.

"Ah!" said he, "it is my friend Mr. Aycon. Bontet, bring me some wine, too, that I may drink with my friend." And he added, addressing me: "You will find our good Bontet most obliging. He is a tenant of mine, and he will do anything to oblige me and my friends. Isn't it so, Bontet?"

The fellow grunted a surly and none too respectful assent, and left the room to fetch the duke his wine. Silence followed on his departure for some seconds. Then the duke came up to where I stood, folded his arms, and looked me full in the face.

"It is difficult to lose the pleasure of your company, sir," he said.

"If you will depart from here alone," I retorted, "you shall find it the easiest thing in the world. For, in truth, it is not desire for your society that brings me here."

He lifted a hand and tugged at his mustache.

"You have, perhaps, been to the convent?" he hazarded.

"I have just come from there," I rejoined.

"I am not an Englishman," said he, curling the end of the mustache, "and I do not know how plain an intimation need be to discourage one of your resolute race. For my part, I should have thought that when a lady accepts the escort of one gentleman, it means that she does not desire that of another."

He said this with a great air and an assumption of dignity that contrasted strongly with the unrestrained paroxysms of the night before. I take it that success--or what seems such--may transform a man as though it changed his very skin. But I was not skilled to cross swords with him in talk of that kind, so I put my hands in my pockets and leaned against the shutter and said bluntly:

"God knows what lies you told her, you see."

His white face suddenly flushed; but he held himself in and retorted with a sneer:

"A disabled right arm gives a man fine courage."

"Nonsense!" said I. "I can aim as well with my left;" and that indeed was not very far from the truth. And I went on: "Is she here?"

"Mme. and Mlle. Delhasse are both here, under my escort."

"I should like to see Mlle. Delhasse," I observed.

He answered me in low tones, but with the passion in him closer to the surface now and near on boiling up through the thin film of his self-restraint:

"So long as I live, you shall never see her."

But I cared not, for my heart leaped in joy at his words. They meant to me that he dared not let me see her; that, be the meaning of her consent to go with him what it might, yet he dared not match his power over her against mine. And whence came the power he feared? It could be mine only if I had touched her heart.

"I presume she may see whom she will," said I still carelessly.

"Her mother will protect her from you with my help."

There was silence for a minute. Then I said:

"I will not leave here without seeing her."

And a pause followed my words till the duke, fixing his eyes on mine, answered significantly:

"If you leave here alive to-night, you are welcome to take her with you."

I understood, and I nodded my head.

"My left arm is as sound as yours," he added; "and, maybe, better practiced."

Our eyes met again, and the agreement was sealed. The duke was about to speak again, when a sudden thought struck me. I put my hand in my pocket and drew out the Cardinal's Necklace. And I flung it on the table before me, saying:

"Let me return that to you, sir."

The duke stood regarding the necklace for a moment, as it lay gleaming and glittering on the wooden table in the bare inn parlor. Then he stepped up to the table, but at the moment I cried:

"You won't steal her away before--before--"

"Before we fight? I will not, on my honor." He paused and added: "For there is one thing I want more even than her."

I could guess what that was.

And then he put out his hand, took up the necklace, and thrust it carelessly into the pocket of his coat. And looking across the room, I saw the inn-keeper, Jacques Bontet, standing in the doorway and staring with all his eyes at the spot on the table where the glittering thing had for a moment lain; and as the fellow set down the wine he had brought for the duke, I swear that he trembled as a man who has seen a ghost; for he spilled some of the wine and chinked the bottle against the glass. But while I stared at him, the duke lifted his glass and bowed to me, saying, with a smile and as though he jested in some phrase of extravagant friendship for me:

"May nothing less than death part you and me?"

And I drank the toast with him, saying "Amen."

CHAPTER XVII.
A Reluctant Intrusion.

As Bontet the inn-keeper set the wine on the table before the Duke of Saint-Maclou, the big clock in the hall of the inn struck noon. It is strange to me, even now when the story has grown old in my memory, to recall all that happened before the hands of that clock pointed again to twelve. And last year when I revisited the neighborhood and found a neat new house standing on the site of the ramshackle inn, I could not pass by without a queer feeling in my throat; for it was there that the results of the duchess' indiscretion finally worked themselves out to their unexpected, fatal, and momentous ending. Seldom, as I should suppose, has such a mixed skein of good and evil, of fatality and happiness, been spun from material no more substantial than a sportive lady's idle freak.

"By the way, Mr. Aycon," said the duke, after we had drunk our toast, "I have had a message from the magistrate at Avranches requesting our presence to-morrow morning at eleven o'clock. An inquiry has to be held into the death of that rascal Lafleur, and our evidence must be taken. It is a mere formality, the magistrate is good enough to assure me, and I have assured him that we shall neither of us allow anything to interfere with our waiting on him, if we can possibly do so."

"I could have sent no other message myself," said I.

"I will also," continued the duke, "send word by Bontet here to those two friends of mine at Pontorson. It would be dull for you to dine alone with me, and, as the evening promises to be fine, I will ask them to be here by five o'clock, and we will have a stroll on the sands and a nearer look at the Mount before our meal. They are officers who are quartered there."

"Their presence," said I, "will add greatly to the pleasure of the evening."

"Meanwhile, if you will excuse me, I shall take an hour or two's rest. We missed our sleep last night, and we should wish to be fresh when our guests arrive. If I might advise you--"

"I am about to breakfast, after that I may follow your advice."

"Ah, you've not breakfasted? You can't do better, then. ***Au revoir***;" and with a bow he left me, calling to Bontet to follow him upstairs and wait for the note which was to go to the officers at Pontorson. It must be admitted that the duke conducted the necessary arrangements with much tact.

In a quarter of an hour my breakfast was before me, and I seated myself with my back to the door and my face to the window. I had plenty to think about as I ate; but my chief anxiety was by some means to obtain an interview with Marie Delhasse, not with a view to persuading her to attempt escape with me before the evening--for I had made up my mind that the issue with the duke must be faced now, once for all--but in the hope of discovering why she had allowed herself to be persuaded into leaving the convent. Until I knew that, I was a prey to wretched doubts and despondency, which even my deep-seated confidence in her could not overcome. Fortunately I had a small sum of money in my pocket, and I felt sure that Bontet's devotion to the duke would not be proof against an adequate bribe: perhaps he would be able to assist me in eluding the vigilance of Madame Delhasse and obtaining speech with her daughter.

Bontet, detained as I supposed by the duke, had left a kitchen-girl to attend on me; but I soon saw him come out into the yard, carrying a letter in his hand. He walked slowly across to the stable door, at which the face, suddenly presented and withdrawn, had caught my attention. He stopped before the door a moment, then the door opened. I could not see whether he opened it or whether it was unlocked from within, for his burly frame obstructed my view; but the pause was long enough to show that more than the lifting of a latch was necessary. And that I thought worth notice. The door closed after Bontet. I rose, opened my window and listened; but the yard was broad and no sound reached me from the stable.

I waited there five minutes perhaps. The inn-keeper did not reappear, so I returned to my place. I had finished my meal before he came out. This time I was tolerably sure that the door was closed behind him by another hand, and I fancied that I heard the click of a lock. Also I noticed that the letter was no longer visible-- of course, he might have put it in his pocket. Jumping up suddenly as though I had just chanced to notice him, I asked him if he were off to Pontorson, or, if not, had he a moment for conversation.

"I am going in a few minutes, sir," he answered; "but I am at your service now."

The words were civil enough, but his manner was surly and suspicious. Lighting a cigarette, I sat down on the window-sill, while he stood just outside.

"I want a bedroom," said I. "Have you one for me?"

"I have given you the room on the first floor, immediately opposite that of the duke."

"Good. And where are the ladies lodged?"

He made no difficulty about giving me an answer.

"They have a sitting room on the first floor," he answered, "but hitherto they have not used it. They have two bedrooms, connected by an interior door, on the second floor, and they have not left them since their arrival."

"Has the duke visited them there?"

"I don't think he has seen them. They had a conversation on their arrival;" and the fellow grinned.

Now was my time. I took a hundred-franc note out of my pocket and held it in my hand so that he could see the figures on it. I hoped that he would not be exorbitant, for I had but one more and some loose napoleons in my pocket.

"What was the conversation about?" I asked.

He put out his hand for the note; but I kept my grasp on it. Honesty was not written large--no, nor plain to read--on Bontet's fat face.

"I heard little of it; but the young lady said, as they hurried upstairs: 'Where is he? Where is he?'"

"Yes, yes!"

And I held out the note to him. He had earned it. And greedily he clutched it, and stowed it in his breeches pocket under his blouse.

"I heard no more; they hurried her up; the old lady had her by one arm and the duke by the other. She looked distressed--why, I know not; for I suppose"--here a sly grin spread over the fellow's face--"that the pretty present I saw is for her."

"It's the property of the duke," I said.

"But gentlemen sometimes make presents to ladies," he suggested.

"It may be his purpose to do so. Bontet, I want to see the young lady."

He laughed insolently, kicking his toe against the wall.

"What use, unless you have a better present, sir? But it's nothing to me. If you can manage it, you're welcome."

"But how am I to manage it? Come, earn your money, and perhaps you'll earn more."

"You're liberal, sir;" and he stared at me as though he were trying to look into my pocket and see how much money was there. I was glad that his glance was not so penetrating. "But I can't help you. Stay, though. The old lady has ordered coffee for two in the sitting-room, and bids me rouse the duke when it is ready: so perhaps the young lady will be left alone for a time. If you could steal up--"

I was not in the mood to stand on a punctilio. My brain was kindled by Marie's words, "Where is he?" Already I was searching for their meaning and finding what I wished. If I could see her, and learn the longed-for truth from her, I should go in good heart to my conflict with the duke.

"Go to your room," said Bontet, whom my prospective *largesse* had persuaded to civility and almost to eagerness, "and wait. If madame and the duke go there, I'll let you know. But you must risk meeting them."

"I don't mind about that," said I; and, in truth, nothing could make my relations with the pair more hostile than they were already.

My business with Bontet was finished; but I indulged my curiosity for a moment.

"You have a good stable over there, I see," I remarked. "How many horses have you there?"

The fellow turned very red: all signs of good humor vanished from his face; my bribe evidently gave me no right to question him on that subject.

"There are no horses there," he grunted. "The horses are in the new stable facing the road. This one is disused."

"Oh, I saw you come out from there, and I thought--"

"I keep some stores there," he said sullenly.

"And that's why it's kept locked?" I asked at a venture.

"Precisely, sir," he replied. But his uneasy air confirmed my suspicions as to the stable. It hid some secret, I was sure. Nay, I began to be sure that my eyes had not played me false, and that I had indeed seen the face I seemed to see. If that were so, friend Bontet was playing a double game and probably enjoying more than one paymaster.

However, I had no leisure to follow that track, nor was I much concerned to attempt the task. The next day would be time--if I were alive the next day: and I cared little if the secret were never revealed. It was nothing to me--for it never crossed my mind that fresh designs might be hatched in the stable. Dismissing the matter, I did as Bontet advised, and walked upstairs to my room; and as luck would have it, I met Mme. Delhasse plump on the landing, she being on her way to the sitting room. I bowed low. Madame gave me a look of hatred and passed by me. As she displayed no surprise, it was evident that the duke had carried or sent word of my arrival. I was not minded to let her go without a word or two.

"Madame--" I began; but she was too quick for me. She burst out in a torrent of angry abuse. Her resentment, dammed so long for want of opportunity, carried her away. To speak soberly and by the card, the woman was a hideous thing to see and hear; for in her wrath at me, she spared not to set forth in unshamed plainness her designs, nor to declare of what rewards, promised by the duke, my interference had gone near to rob her and still rendered uncertain. Her voice rose, for all her efforts to keep it low, and she mingled foul words of the duchess and of me with scornful curses on the virtue of her daughter. I could say nothing; I stood there wondering that such creatures lived, amazed that Marie Delhasse must call such an one her mother.

Then in the midst of her tirade, the duke, roused without Bontet's help, came out of his room, and waited a moment listening to the flow of the torrent. And, strange as it seemed, he smiled at me and shrugged his shoulders, and I found myself smiling also; for disgusting as the woman was, she was amusing, too. And the duke went and caught her by the shoulder and said:

"Come, don't be silly, mother. We can settle our accounts with Mr. Aycon in another way than this."

His touch and words seemed to sober her--or perhaps her passion had run its course. She turned to him, and her lips parted with a smile, a cunning and--if my opinion be asked--loathsome smile; and she caressed the lapel of his coat with her hand. And the duke, who was smoking, smoked on, so that the smoke blew in her face, and she coughed and choked: whereat the duke also smiled. He set the right value on his instrument, and took pleasure in showing how he despised her.

"My dear, dear duke, I have such news for you--such news?" she said, ignoring, as perforce she must, his rudeness. "Come in here, and leave that man."

At this the duke suddenly bent forward, his scornful, insolent toleration giving place to interest.

"News?" he cried, and he drew her toward the door to which she had been going, neither of them paying any more attention to me. And the door closed upon them.

The duke had not needed Bontet's rousing. I did not need Bontet to tell me that the coast was clear. With a last alert glance at the door, I trod softly across the landing and reached the stairs by which Mlle. Delhasse had descended. Gently I mounted, and on reaching the top of the flight found a door directly facing me. I turned the handle, but the door was locked. I rattled the handle cautiously--and then again, and again. And presently I heard a light, timid, hesitating step inside; and through the door came, in the voice of Marie Delhasse:

"Who's there?"

And I answered at once, boldly, but in a low voice:

"It is I. Open the door."

She, in her turn, knew my voice; for the door was opened, and Marie Delhasse stood before me, her face pale with weariness and sorrow, and her eyes wide with wonder. She drew back before me, and I stepped in and shut the door, finding myself in a rather large, sparely furnished room. A door opposite was half-open. On the bed lay a bonnet and a jacket which certainly did not belong to Marie.

Most undoubtedly I had intruded into the bedchamber of that highly respectable lady, Mme. Delhasse. I can only plead that the circumstances were peculiar.

CHAPTER XVIII.
A Strange Good Humor.

For a moment Marie Delhasse stood looking at me; then she uttered a low cry, full of relief, of security, of joy; and coming to me stretched out her hands, saying:

"You are here then, after all!"

Charmed to see how she greeted me, I had not the heart to tell her that her peril was not past; nor did she give me the opportunity, for went on directly:

"And you are wounded? But not badly, not badly, Mr. Aycon?"

"Who told you I was wounded?"

"Why, the duke. He said that you had been shot by a thief, and were very badly hurt; and--and--" She stopped, blushing.

("Where is he?" I remembered the words; my forecast of their meaning had been true.)

"And did what he told you," I asked softly, "make you leave the convent and come to find me?"

"Yes," she answered, taking courage and meeting my eyes. "And then you were not here, and I thought it was a trap."

"You were right; it was a trap. I came to find you at the convent, but you were gone: only by the chance of meeting with a friend who saw the duke's carriage standing here have I found you."

"You were seeking for me?"

"Yes, I was seeking for you."

I spoke slowly, as though hours were open for our talk; but suddenly I remembered that at any moment the old witch might return. And I had much to say before she came.

"Marie--" I began eagerly, never thinking that the name she had come to bear in my thoughts could be new and strange from my lips. But the moment I had uttered it I perceived what I had done, for she drew back further, gazing at me with inquiring eyes, and her breath seemed arrested. Then, answering the question in her eyes, I said simply:

"For what else am I here, Marie?" and I caught her hand in my left hand.

She stood motionless, still silently asking what I would. And I kissed her hand. And again the low cry, lower still--half a cry and half a sigh--came from her, and she drew timidly nearer to me; and I drew her yet nearer, whispering, in a broken word or two, that I loved her.

But she, still dazed, looked up at me, whispering, "When, when?"

And I could not tell her when I had come to love her, for I did not know then--nor can I recollect now; nor have I any opinion about it, save that it speaks ill for me that it was not when first I set my eyes upon her. But she doubted, remembering that I had seemed fancy-struck with the little duchess, and cold, maybe stern, to her; and because, I think, she knew that I had seen her tempted. And to silence her doubts, I kissed her lips. She did not return my kiss, but stood with wondering eyes. Then in an instant a change came over her face. I felt her press my hand, and for an instant or two her lips moved, but I heard no words, nor do I think that the unheard words were for my ear; and I bowed my head.

Yet time pressed. Again I collected my thoughts from this sweet reverie--wherein what gave me not least joy was the perfect trust she showed in me, for that is perhaps the one thing in this world that a man may be proud to win--and said to her:

"Marie, you must listen. I have something to tell you."

"Oh, you'll take me away from them?" she cried, clutching my hand in both of hers.

"I can't now," I answered. "You must be brave. Listen: if I try to take you away now, it may be that I should be killed and you left defenseless. But this evening you can be safe, whatever befalls me."

"Why, what should befall you?" she asked, with a swift movement that brought her closer to me.

I had to tell her the truth, or my plan for her salvation would not be carried out.

"To-night I fight the duke. Hush! hush! Yes, I must fight with the duke--yes, wounded arm, my darling, notwithstanding. We shall leave here about five and go down to the bay toward the Mount, and there on the sands we shall fight. And-- listen now--you must follow us, about half an hour after we have gone."

"But they will not let me go."

"Go you must. Marie, here is a pistol. Take it; and if anyone stops you, use it. But I think none will; for the duke will be with me, and I do not think Bontet will interfere."

"But my mother?"

"You are as strong as she."

"Yes, yes, I'll come. You'll be on the sands; I'll come!" The help she had found in me made her brave now.

"You will get there as we are fighting or soon after. Do not look for me or for the duke, but look for two gentlemen whom you do not know, they will be there-- French officers--and to their honor you must trust."

"But why not to you?"

"If I am alive and well, I shall not fail you; but if I come not, go to them and demand their protection from the duke, telling them how he has snared you here. And they will not suffer him to carry you off against your will. Do you see? Do you understand?"

"Yes, I see. But must you fight?"

"Yes, dear, I must fight. The duke will not trouble you again, I think, before the evening; and if you remember what I have told you, all will be well."

So I tried to comfort her, believing as I did that no two French gentlemen would desire or dare to refuse her their protection against the duke. But she was clinging to me now, in great distress that I must fight--and indeed I had rather have fought at another time myself--and in fresh terror of her mother's anger, seeing that I should not be there to bear it for her.

"For," she said, "we have had a terrible quarrel just before you came. I told her that unless I saw you within an hour nothing but force should keep me here, and that if they kept me here by force, I would find means to kill myself; and that I would not see nor speak to the duke unless he brought me to you, according to his promise; and that if he sent his necklace again--for he sent it here half an hour ago--I would not send it back as I did then, but would fling it out of the window yonder into the cattle pond, where he could go and fetch it out himself."

And my dearest Marie, finding increased courage from reciting her courageous speech, and from my friendly hearing of it, raised her voice, and her eyes flashed, so that she looked yet more beautiful; and again did I forget inexorable time. But it struck me that there was small wonder that Mme. Delhasse's temper had not been of the best nor calculated to endure patiently such a vexatious encounter as befell her when she ran against me on the landing outside her door.

Yet Marie's courage failed again; and I told her that before we fought I would tell my second of her state, so that if she came not and I were wounded (of worse I did not speak), he would come to the inn and bring her to me. And this comforted her more, so that she grew calmer, and, passing from our present difficulties, she gave herself to persuading me (nor would the poor girl believe that I needed no persuading) that in no case would she have yielded to the duke, and that her mother had left her in wrath born of an utter despair that Marie's will in the matter could ever be broken down.

"For I told her," Marie repeated, "that I would sooner die!"

She paused, and raising her eyes to mine, said to me (and here I think courage was not lacking in her):

"Yes, although once I had hesitated, now I had rather die. For when I hesitated, God sent you to my door, that in love I might find salvation."

Well, I do not know that a man does well to describe all that passes at times like this. There are things rather meet to be left dwelling in his own heart, sweetening all his life, and causing him to marvel that sinners have such joys conceded to them this side of Heaven; so that in their recollection he may find, mingling with his delight, an occasion for humility such as it little harms any of us to light on now and then.

Enough then--for the telling of it; but enough in the passing of it there was not nor could be. Yet at last, because needs must when the devil--or a son--aye, or an elderly daughter of his--drives, I found myself outside the door of Mme. Delhasse's room. With the turning of the lock Marie whispered a last word to me, and full of hope I turned to descend the stairs. For I had upon me the feeling which, oftener perhaps than we think, gave to the righteous cause a victory against odds when ordeal of battle held sway. Now, such a feeling is, I take it, of small use in a court of law.

But Fortune lost no time in checking my presumption by an accident which at first gave me great concern. For, even as I turned away from the door of the room, there was Mme. Delhasse coming up the stairs. I was fairly caught, there was no doubt about it; and for Marie's sake I was deeply grieved, for I feared that my discovery would mean another stormy scene for her. Nevertheless, to make the best of it, I assumed a jaunty air as I said to Mlle. Delhasse:

"The duke will be witness that you were not in your room, madame. You will not be compromised."

I fully expected that an outburst of anger would follow on this pleasantry of mine--which was, I confess, rather in the taste best suited to Mme. Delhasse than in the best as judged by an abstract standard--but to my surprise the old creature did nothing worse than bestow on me a sour grin. Apparently, if I were well-pleased with the last half-hour, she had found time pass no less pleasantly. All traces of her exasperation and ill humor had gone, and she looked as pleased and contented as though she had been an exemplary mother, rewarded (as such deserve to be) by complete love and peace in her family circle.

"You've been slinking in behind my back, have you?" she asked, but still with a grin.

"It would have been rude to force an entrance to your face," I observed.

"And I suppose you've been making love to the girl?"

"At the proper time, madame," said I, with much courtesy, "I shall no doubt ask you for an interview with regard to that matter. I shall omit no respect that you deserve."

As I spoke, I stood on one side to let her pass. I cannot make up my mind whether her recent fury or her present good humor repelled me more.

"You'd have a fine fool for a wife," said she, with a jerk of her thumb toward the room where the daughter was.

"I should be compensated by a very clever mother-in-law," said I.

The old woman paused for an instant at the top of the stairs, and looked me up and down.

"Aye," said she, "you men think yourselves mighty clever, but a woman gets the better of you all now and then."

I was utterly puzzled by her evident exultation. The duke could not have consented to accept her society in place of her daughter's; but I risked the impropriety and hazarded the suggestion to Mme. Delhasse. Her face curled in cunning wrinkles. She seemed to be about to speak, but then she shut her lips with a snap, and suspicion betrayed itself again in her eyes. She had a secret--a fresh secret--I could have sworn, and in her triumph she had come near to saying something that might have cast light on it.

"By the way," I said, "your daughter did not expect my coming." It was perhaps a vain hope, but I thought that I might save Marie from a tirade.

The old woman shrugged her shoulders, and observed carelessly:

"The fool may do what she likes;" and with this she knocked at the door.

I did not wait to see it opened--to confess the truth, I felt not sure of my temper were I forced to see her and Marie together--but went downstairs and into my own room. There I sat down in a chair by the window close to a small table, for I meant to write a letter or two to friends at home, in case the duke's left hand should prove more skillful than mine when we met that evening. But, finding that I could hardly write with my right hand and couldn't write at all with the other, I contented myself with scrawling laboriously a short note to Gustave de Berensac, which I put in my pocket, having indorsed on it a direction for its delivery in case I should meet with an accident. Then I lay back in my chair, regretting, I recollect, that, as my luggage was left at Avranches, I had not a clean shirt to fight in; and then, becoming drowsy, I began to stare idly along the road in front of the window, rehearsing the events of the last few days in my mind, but coming back to Marie Delhasse.

So an hour passed away. Then I rose and stretched myself, and gave a glance out of the window to see if we were likely to have a fine evening for our sport, for clouds had been gathering up all day. And when I had made up my mind that the rain would hold off long enough for our purpose, I looked down at the road again, and there I saw two figures which I knew. From the direction of Pontorson came Jacques Bontet the inn-keeper, slouching along and smoking a thin black cigar.

"Ah! he has been to deliver the note to our friends the officers," said I to myself.

And then I looked at the other familiar figure, which was that of Mme. Delhasse. She wore the bonnet and cloak which had been lying on the bed in her room at the time of my intrusion. She was just leaving the premises of the inn strolling, nay dawdling, along. She met Bontet and stopped for a moment in conversation with him. Then she pursued her leisurely walk in the direction of Pontorson, and I watched her till she was about three hundred yards off. But her form had no charms, and, growing tired of the prospect, I turned away remarking to myself:

"I suppose the old lady wants just a little stroll before dinner."

Nor did I see any reason to be dissatisfied with either of my inferences--at the moment. So I disturbed myself no more, but rang the bell and ordered some coffee and a little glass of the least bad brandy in the inn. For it could not be long before I was presented with the Duke of Saint-Maclou's compliments and an intimation that he would be glad to have my company on a walk in the cool of the evening.

CHAPTER XIX.
Unsummoned Witnesses.

Slowly the afternoon wore away. My content had given place to urgent impatience, and I longed every moment for the summons to action. None came; and a quarter to five I went downstairs, hoping to find some means of whiling away the interval of time. Pushing open the door of the little salle-à-manger, I was presented with a back view of my host M. Bontet, who was leaning out of the window. Just as I entered, he shouted "Ready at six!" Then he turned swiftly round, having, I suppose, heard my entrance; at the same moment, the sound of a door violently slammed struck on my ear across the yard. I moved quickly up to the window. The stable door was shut; and Bontet faced me with a surly frown on his brow.

"What is to be ready at six?" I asked.

"Some refreshments for Mme. Delhasse," he answered readily.

"You order refreshments from the stable?"

"I was shouting to the scullery: the door is, as you will perceive, sir, there to the left."

Now I knew that this was a lie, and I might very likely have said as much, had not the Duke of Saint-Maclou at this moment come into the room. He bowed to me, but addressed himself to Bontet.

"Well, are the gentlemen to be here at five?" he asked.

Bontet, with an air of relief, began an explanation. One of the gentlemen--M. de Vieuville, he believed--had read out the note in his presence, and had desired him to tell the duke that he and the other gentleman would meet the duke and his friend on the sands at a quarter to six. They would be where the road ceased and the sand began at that hour.

"He seems to think," Bontet explained, "that less attention would thus be directed to the affair."

The precaution seemed wise enough; but why had M. de Vieuville taken Bontet so much into his confidence? The same thought struck the duke, for he asked sharply:

"Why did he read the note to you?"

"Oh, he thought nothing of that," said Bontet easily. "The gentlemen at Pontorson know me very well: several affairs have been arranged from this house."

"You ought to keep a private cemetery," said the duke with a grim smile.

"The sands are there," laughed the fellow, with a wave of his hand.

Nobody appeared to desire to continue this cheerful conversation, and silence fell upon us for some moments. Then the duke observed:

"Bontet, I want you for a few minutes. Mr. Aycon, shall you be ready to start in half an hour? Our friends will probably bring pistols: failing that, I can provide you, if you have no objection to using mine."

I bowed, and they left me alone. And then, having nothing better to do, I lit a cigar, vaulted out of the window, and strolled toward the stable. My curiosity about the stable had been growing rapidly. I cast a glance round, and saw nobody in the yard. Then, with a careless air, I turned the handle of the door. Nothing occurred. I turned it more violently; still nothing happened. I bent down suddenly and looked through the keyhole. And I saw--not a key, but--an eye! And for ten seconds I looked at the eye. Then the eye disappeared; and I heard that little unmistakable "click." The eye had a pistol--and had cocked it! Was that because it saw through the keyhole strange garments, instead of the friendly bright blue of Bontet's blouse? And why had the eye such a dislike to strangers? I straightened myself again and took a walk along the length of the stable, considering these questions and, incidentally, looking for a window; but the only window was a clear four feet above my head.

I am puzzled even now to say whether I regret not having listened to the suspicion that was strong in my breast. Had I forecast, in the least degree, the result of my neglecting to pay heed to its warning, I should not have hesitated for a moment. But in the absence of such a presage, I felt rather indifferent about the matter. My predominant desire was to avoid the necessity of postponing the settlement of the issue between the duke and myself; and a delay to that must needs follow, if I took action in regard to the stable. Moreover, why should I stir in the matter? I had a right to waive any grievance of my own; for the rest, it seemed to me that justice was not much concerned in the matter; the merits or demerits of the parties were, in my view, pretty equal; and I questioned the obligation to incur, not only the delay which I detested, but, in all probability, a very risky adventure in a cause which I had very little at heart.

If "the eye" could, by being "ready at six," get out of the stable while the duke and I were engaged otherwise and elsewhere, why--"Let him," said I, "and go to the devil his own way. He's sure to get there at last!" So I reasoned--or perhaps, I should rather say, so I felt; and I must repeat that I find it difficult now to be very sorry that my mood was what it was.

My half hour was passing. I crossed back to the window and got in again. The duke, whose impatience rivaled my own, was waiting for me. A case of pistols lay on the table and, having held them up for me to see, he slipped them inside his coat.

"Are you ready, sir?" he asked. "We may as well be starting."

I bowed and motioned him to precede me. He also, in spite of his impatience, seemed to me to be in a better humor than earlier in the day. The interview with Mme. Delhasse must have been satisfactory to both parties. Had not his face showed me the improvement in his temper, his first words after we left the premises of the inn (at a quarter past five exactly) would have declared it; for he turned to me and said:

"Look here, Mr. Aycon. You're running a great risk for nothing. Be a sensible man. Go back to Avranches, thence to Cherbourg, and thence to where you live-- and leave me to settle my own affairs."

"Before I accept that proposal," said I, "I must know what 'your own affairs' include."

"You're making a fool of yourself--or being made a fool of--which you please," he assured me; and his face wore for the moment an almost friendly look. I saw clearly that he believed he had won the day. The old lady had managed to make him think that--by what artifice I knew not. But what I did know was that I believed not a jot of the insinuation he was conveying to me, and had not a doubt of the truth, and sincerity of Marie Delhasse.

"The best of us do that sometimes," I answered. "And when one has begun, it is best to go through."

"As you please. Have you ever practiced with your left hand?"

"No," said I.

"Then," said he, "you've not long to live."

To do him justice, he said it in no boasting way, but like a man who would warn me, and earnestly.

"I have never practiced with my right either," I remarked. "I think I get rather a pull by the arrangement."

He walked on in silence for a few yards. Then he asked:

"You're resolved on it?"

"Absolutely," I returned. For I understood that he did but offer the same terms as before--terms which included the abandonment of Marie Delhasse.

On we went, our faces set toward the great Mount, and with the sinking sun on our left hands. We met few people, and as we reached the sands yet fewer. When we came to a stand, just where the causeway now begins (it was not built then), nobody was in sight. The duke took out his watch.

"We are punctual to the minute," said he. "I hope those fellows won't be very late, or the best of the light will be gone."

There were some large flat blocks of stone lying by the roadside, and we sat down on them and waited. We were both smoking, and we found little to say to one another. For my part, I thought less of our coming encounter than of the success of the scheme which I had laid for Marie's safety. And I believe that the duke, on his part, gave equally small heed to the fight; for the smile of triumph or satisfaction flitted now and again across his face, called forth, I made no doubt, by the pleasant conviction which Mlle. Delhasse had instilled into his mind, and which had caused him to dub me a fool for risking my life in the service of a woman who had promised all he asked of her.

But the sun sank; the best of the light went; and the officers from Pontorson did not come. It was hard on six.

"If we fight to-night, we must fight now!" cried the duke suddenly. "What the plague has become of the fellows?"

"It's not too dark for me," said I.

"But it soon will be for me," he answered. "Come, are we to wait till to-morrow?"

"We'll wait till to-morrow," said I, "if you'll promise not to seek to see or speak to Mlle. Delhasse till to-morrow. Otherwise we'll fight tonight, seconds or no seconds, light or no light!"

I never understood perfectly the temper of the man, nor the sudden gusts of passion to which, at a word that chanced to touch him, he was subject. Such a storm caught him now, and he bounded up from where he sat, cursing me for an insolent fellow who dared to put him under terms--for a fool who flattered himself that all women loved him--and for many other things which it is not well to repeat. So that at last I said:

"Lead the way, then: you know the best place, I suppose."

Still muttering in fury, cursing now me, now the neglectful seconds, he strode rapidly on to the sands and led the way at a quick pace, walking nearly toward the setting sun. The land trended the least bit outward here, and the direction kept us well under the lee of a rough stone wall that fringed the sands on the landward side. Stunted bushes raised their heads above the wall, and the whole made a perfect screen. Thus we walked for some ten minutes with the sun in our eyes and the murmur of the sea in our ears. Then at a spot where the bushes rose highest the duke abruptly stopped, saying, "Here," and took the case of pistols out of his pocket. He examined the loading, handing each in turn to me. While this was being done neither of us spoke. Then he held them both out, the stocks towards me; and I took the one nearest to my hand. The duke laid the other down on the sands and motioned me to follow his example; and he took his handkerchief out of his pocket and wound it round his right hand, confining the fingers closely.

"Tie the knot, if you can," said he, holding out his hand thus bound.

"So far I am willing to trust you," said I; but he bowed ironically as he answered:

"It will be awkward enough anyhow for the one of us that chances to kill the other, seeing that we have no seconds or witnesses; but it would look too black against me, if my right hand were free while yours is in a sling. So pray, Mr. Aycon, do not insist on trusting me too much, but tie the knot if your wounded arm will let you."

Engrossed with my thoughts and my schemes, I had not dwelt on the danger to which he called my attention, and I admit that I hesitated.

"I have no wish to be called a murderer," said I. "Shall we not wait again for M. de Vieuville and his friend?"

"Curse them!" said he, fury in his eye again. "By Heavens, if I live, I'll have a word with them for playing me such a trick! The light is all but gone now. Come, take your place. There is little choice."

"You mean to fight, then?"

"Not if you will leave me in peace: but if not--"

"Let us go back to the inn and fight to-morrow: and meanwhile things shall stand as they are," said I, repeating my offer, in the hope that he would now be more reasonable.

He looked at me sullenly; then his rage came again upon him, and he cried:

"Take your place: stand where you like, and, in God's name, be quick!" And he paused, and then added: "I cannot live another night--" And he broke off again, and finished by crying: "Quick! Are you ready?"

Seeing there was no help for it, I took up a position. No more words passed between us, but with a gesture he signed to me to move a little: and thus he adjusted our places till we were opposite one another, about two yards between us, and each presenting his side direct to the sun, so that its slanting rays troubled each of us equally, and that but little. Then he said:

"I will step back five paces, and do you do the like. When we are at the distance, do you count slowly, 'One--two--three,' and at 'Three' we will fire."

I did not like having to count, but it was necessary that one of us should; and he, when I pressed him, would not. Therefore it was arranged as he said. And I began to step back, but for an instant he stayed me. He was calm now, and he spoke in quiet tones.

"Even now, if you will go!" said he. "For the girl is mine; and I think that, and not my life or death, is what you care about."

"The girl is not yours and never will be," said I. But then I remembered that, the seconds not having come, my scheme had gone astray, and that if he lived in strength, Marie would be well-nigh at his mercy. And on that I grew stern, and the desire for his blood came on me; and he, I think, saw it in my face, for he smiled, and without more turned and walked to his place. And I did the like; and we turned round again and stood facing one another.

All this time my pistol had hung in the fingers of my right hand. I took it now in my left, and looked to it, and cried to the duke:

"Are you ready?"

And he answered easily:

"Yes, I'm ready."

Then I raised my arm and took my aim,--and if the aim were not true on his heart, my hand and not my will deserves the praise of Mercy,--and I cried aloud:

"One!" and paused; and cried "Two!"

And as the word left my lips--before the final fatal "Three!" was so much as ready to my tongue--while I yet looked at the duke to see that I was not taking him unawares--loud and sharp two shots rang out at the same instant in the still air: I felt the whizz of a bullet, as it shaved my ear; and the duke, without a sound, fell forward on the sands, his pistol exploding as he fell.

After all we had our witnesses!

CHAPTER XX.
The Duke's Epitaph.

For a moment I stood in amazement, gazing at my opponent where he lay prostrate on the sands. Then, guided by the smoke which issued from the bushes, I darted across to the low stone wall and vaulted on to the top of it. I dived into the bushes, parting them with head and hand: I was conscious of a man's form rushing by me, but I could pay no heed to him, for right in front of me, in the act of re-loading his pistol, I saw the burly inn-keeper Jacques Bontet. When his eyes fell on me, as I leaped out almost at his very feet, he swore an oath and turned to run. I raised my hand and fired. Alas! the Duke of Saint-Maclou had been justified in his confidence; for, to speak honestly, I do not believe my bullet went within a yard of the fugitive. Hearing the shot and knowing himself unhurt, he halted and faced me. There was no time for re-loading. I took my pistol by the muzzle and ran at him. My right arm was nearly useless; but I took it out of the sling and had it ready, for what it was worth. I saw that the fellow's face was pale and that he displayed no pleasure in the game. But he stood his ground; and I, made wary by the recollection of my maimed state, would not rush on him, but came to a stand about a yard from him, reconnoitering how I might best spring on him. Thus we rested for a moment till remembering that the duke, if he were not already dead, lay at the mercy of the other scoundrel, I gathered myself together and threw myself at Jacques Bontet. He also had clubbed his weapon, and he struck wildly at me as I came on. My head he missed, and the blow fell on my right shoulder, settling once for all the question whether my right arm was to be of any use or not. Yet its uselessness mattered not, for I countered his blow with a better, and the butt of my pistol fell full and square on his forehead. For a moment he stood looking at me, with hatred and fear in his eyes: then, as it seemed to me, quite slowly his knees gave way under him; his face dropped down from mine; he might have been sinking into the ground, till at last, his knees being bent right under him, uttering a low groan, he toppled over and lay on the ground.

Spending on him and his state no more thought that they deserved, I snatched his pistol from him (for mine was broken at the junction of barrel and stock), and, without waiting to load (and indeed with one hand helpless and in the agitation which I was suffering it would have taken me more than a moment), I hastened back to the wall, and, parting the bushes, looked over. It was a strange sight that I saw. The duke was no longer prone on his face, as he had fallen, but lay on his back, with his arms stretched out, crosswise; and by his side knelt a small spare man, who searched, hunted, and rummaged with hasty, yet cool and methodical, touch, every inch of his clothing. Up and down, across and across, into every pocket, along every lining, aye, down to the boots, ran the nimble fingers; and in the still of the evening, which seemed not broken but rather emphasized by the rumble of the tide that had begun to come in over the sands from the Mount, his passionate curses struck my ears. I recollect that I smiled--nay, I believe that I laughed--for the man was my old acquaintance Pierre--and Pierre was still on the track of the Cardinal's Necklace; and he had not doubted, any more than I had doubted, that the duke carried it upon his person. Yet Pierre found it not, for he was growing angry now; he seemed to worry the still body, pushing it and tossing the arms of it to and fro as a puppy tosses a slipper or a cushion. And all the while the unconscious face of the Duke of Saint-Maclou was turned up to heaven, and a stiff smile seemed to mock the baffled plunderer. And I also wondered where the necklace was.

Then I let myself down on to the noiseless sands and stole across to the spot where the pair were. Pierre's hands were searching desperately and wildly now; he no longer expected to find, but he could not yet believe that the search was in very truth in vain. Absorbed in his task, he heard me not; and coming up I set my foot on the pistol that lay by him, and caught him, as the duke had caught Lafleur his comrade, by the nape of the neck, and said to him, in a bantering tone:

"Well, is it not there, my friend?"

He wriggled; but the strength of the little man in a struggle at close quarters was as nothing, and I held him easily with my one sound hand. And I mocked him, exhorting him to look again, telling him that everything was not to be seen from a stable, and bidding him call Lafleur from hell to help him. And under my grip he grew quiet and ceased to search; and I heard nothing but his quick breathing. And I laughed at him as I plucked him off the duke and flung him on his back on the sands, and stood looking down on him. But he asked no mercy of me; his small eyes answered defiance back to me, and he glanced still wistfully at the quiet man beside us.

Yet he was to escape me--with small pain to me, I confess. For at the moment a cry rang loud in my ear: I knew the voice; and though I kept my foot on Pierre's pistol, yet I turned my head. And on the instant the fellow sprang to his feet, and, with an agility that I could not have matched, started running across the sands to-ward the Mount. Before I had realized what he was about, he had thirty yards' start of me. I heard the water rushing in now; he must wade deep, nay, he must swim to win the Mount. But from me he was safe, for I was no such runner as he. Yet, had he and I been alone, I would have pursued him. But the cry rang out again, and, giving no more thought to him, I turned whither Marie Delhasse, come in pursuance of my directions, stood with a hand pointed in questioning at the duke, and the pistol that I had given her fallen from her fingers on the sand. And she swayed to and fro, till I set my arm round her and steadied her.

"Have you killed him?" she asked in a frightened whisper.

"I did not so much as fire at him," I answered. "We were attacked by thieves."

"By thieves?"

"The inn-keeper and another. They thought that he carried the necklace, and tracked us here."

"And did they take it?"

"It was not on him," I answered, looking into her eyes.

She raised them to mine and said simply:

"I have it not;" and with that, asking no more, she drew near to the duke, and sat down by him on the sand, and lifted his head on to her lap, and wiped his brow with her handkerchief, saying in a low voice, "Is he dead?"

Now, whether it be, as some say, that the voice a man loves will rouse him when none else will, or that the duke's swoon had merely come to its natural end, I know not; but, as she spoke, he, who had slept through Pierre's rough handling, opened his eyes, and, seeing where he was, tried to raise his hand, groping after hers: and he spoke, with difficulty indeed, yet plainly enough, saying:

"The rascals thought I had the necklace. They did not know how kind you had been, my darling."

I started where I stood. Marie grew red and then white, and looked down at him no longer with pity, but with scorn and anger on her face.

"I have it not," she said again. "For all heaven, I would not touch it!"

And she looked up to me as she said it, praying me with her eyes to believe.

But her words roused and stung the duke to an effort and an activity that I thought impossible to him; for he rolled himself from her lap, and, raising himself on his hand, with half his body lifted from the ground, said in a loud voice:

"You have it not? You haven't the necklace? Why, your message told me that you would never part from it again?"

"I sent no message," she answered in a hard voice, devoid of pity for him; how should she pity him? "I sent no message, save that I would sooner die than see you again."

Amazement spread over his face even in the hour of his agony.

"You sent," said he, "to say that you would await me to-night, and to ask for the necklace to adorn yourself for my coming."

Though he was dying, I could hardly control myself to hear him speak such words. But Marie, in the same calm scornful voice asked:

"By whom did the message come?"

"By your mother," said he, gazing at her eagerly. "And I sent mine--the one I told you--by her. Marie, was it not true?" he cried, dragging himself nearer to her.

"True!" she echoed--and no more.

But it was enough. For an instant he glared at her; then he cried:

"That old fiend has played a trick on me! She has got the necklace!"

And I began to understand the smile that I had seen on Mme. Delhasse's face, and her marvelous good humor; and I began to have my opinion concerning her evening stroll to Pontorson. Bontet and Pierre had been matched against more than they thought.

The duke, painfully supported on his hand, drew nearer still to Marie; but she rose to her feet and retreated a pace as he advanced. And he said:

"But you love me, Marie? You would have--"

She interrupted him.

"Above all men I loathe you!" she said, looking on him with shrinking and horror in her face.

His wound was heavy on him--he was shot in the stomach and was bleeding inwardly--and had drawn his features; his pain brought a sweat on his brow, and his arm, trembling, scarce held him. Yet none of these things made the anguish in his eyes as he looked at her.

"This is the man I love," said she in calm relentlessness.

And she put out her hand and took mine, and drew me to her, passing her arm through mine. The Duke of Saint-Maclou looked up at us; then he dropped his head, heavily and with a thud on the sand, and so lay till we thought he was dead.

Yet it might be that his life could be saved, and I said to Marie:

"Stay by him, while I run for help."

"I will not stay by him," she said.

"Then do you go," said I. "Stop the first people you meet; or, if you see none, go to the inn. And bid them bring help to carry a wounded man and procure a doctor."

She nodded her head, and, without a glance at him, started running along the sands toward the road. And I, left alone with him, sat down and raised him, as well as I could, turning his face upward again and resting it on my thigh. And I wiped his brow. And, after a time, he opened his eyes.

"Help will be here soon," I said. "She has gone to bring help."

Full ten minutes passed slowly; he lay breathing with difficulty, and from time to time I wiped his brow. At last he spoke.

"There's some brandy in my pocket. Give it me," he said.

I found the flask and gave him some of its contents, which kept the life in him for a little longer. And I was glad to feel that he settled himself, as though more comfortably, against me.

"What happened?" he asked very faintly.

And I told him what had happened, as I conceived it--how that Bontet must have given shelter to Pierre, till such time as escape might be possible; but how that, when Bontet discovered that the necklace was in the inn, the two scoundrels, thinking that they might as well be hanged for a sheep as for a lamb, had determined to make another attempt to secure the coveted spoil; how, in pursuance of this scheme, Bontet had, as I believed, suppressed the duke's message to his friends at Pontorson, with the intent to attack us, as they had done, on the sands; and I added that he himself knew, better than I, what was likely to have become of the necklace in the hands of Mme. Delhasse.

"For my part," I concluded, "I doubt if Madame will be at the inn to welcome us on our return."

"She came to me and told me that Marie would give all I asked, and I gave her the necklace to give to Marie; and believing what she told me, I was anxious not to fight you, for I thought you had nothing to gain by fighting. Yet you angered me, so I resolved to fight."

He seemed to have strength for nothing more; yet at the end, before life left him, one strange last change came over him. Both his rough passion and the terrible abasement of defeat seemed to leave him, and his face became again the face of a well-bred, self-controlled man. There was a helpless effort at a shrug of his shoulders, a scornful slight smile on his lips, and a look of recognition, almost of friendliness, almost of humor, in his eyes, as he said to me, who still held his head:

"Mon Dieu, but I've made a mess of it, Mr. Aycon!"

And I do not know that anyone could better this epitaph which the Duke of Saint-Maclou composed for himself in the last words he spoke this side the grave.

CHAPTER XXI.
A Passing Carriage.

When I saw that the Duke of Saint-Maclou was dead, I laid him down on the sands, straightening him into a seemly posture; and I closed his eyes and spread his handkerchief over his face. Then I began to walk up and down with folded arms, pondering over the life and fate of the man and the strange link between us which the influence of two women had forged. And I recognized also that an hour ago the greater likelihood had been that I should be where he lay, and he be looking down on me. ***Dis aliter visum.*** His own sin had stretched him there, and I lived to muse on the wreck--on the "mess" as he said in self-mockery--that he had made of his life. Yet, as I had felt when I talked to him before, so I felt now, that his had been the hand to open my eyes, and from his mighty but base love I had learned a love as strong and, as I could in all honesty say, more pure.

The sun was quite gone now, the roll of the tide was nearer, and water gleamed between us and the Mount. But we were beyond its utmost rise, save at a spring tide, and I waited long, too engrossed in my thoughts to be impatient for Marie's return. I did not even cross the wall to see how Bontet fared under the blow I had given him--whether he were dead, or lay still stunned, or had found life enough to crawl away. In truth, I cared not then.

Presently across the sands, through the growing gloom, I saw a group approaching me. Marie I knew by her figure and gait and saw more plainly, for she walked a little in front as though she were setting the example of haste. The rest followed together; and, looking past them, I could just discern a carriage which had been driven some way on to the sands. One of the strangers wore top-boots and the livery of a servant. As they approached, he fell back, and the remaining two--a man and a woman on his arm--came more clearly into view. Marie reached me some twenty yards ahead of them.

"I met no one till I was at the inn," she said, "and then this carriage was driving by; and I told them that a gentleman lay hurt on the sands, and they came to help you to carry him up."

I nodded and walked forward to meet them; for by now I knew the man, yes, and the woman, though she wore a veil. And it was too late to stop their approach. Uncovering my head, I stepped up to them, and they stopped in surprise at seeing me. For the pair were Gustave de Berensac and the duchess. He had gone, as he told me afterward, to see the duchess, and they had spent the afternoon in a drive, and she was going to set him down at his friend's quarters in Pontorson, when Marie met them, and not knowing them nor they her (though Gustave had once, two years before, heard her sing) had brought them on this errand.

The little duchess threw up her veil. Her face was pale, her lips quivered, and her eyes asked a trembling question. At the sight of me I think she knew at once what the truth was: it needed but the sight of me to let light in on the seemingly obscure story which Marie had told, of a duel planned, and then interrupted by a treacherous assault and attempted robbery. With my hand I signed to the duchess to stop; but she did not stop, but walked past me, merely asking:

"Is he badly hurt?"

I caught her by the arm and held her.

"Yes," said I, "badly;" and I felt her eyes fixed on mine.

Then she said, gently and calmly:

"Then he is dead?"

"Yes, he is dead," I answered, and loosed her arm.

Gustave de Berensac had not spoken: and he now came silently to my side, and he and I followed a pace or two behind the duchess. The servant had halted ten or fifteen yards away. Marie had reached where the duke lay and stood now close by him, her arms at her side and her head bowed. The duchess walked up to her husband and, kneeling beside him, lifted the handkerchief from his face. The expression wherewith he had spoken his epitaph--the summary of his life--was set on his face, so that he seemed still to smile in bitter amusement. And the little duchess looked long on the face that smiled in contempt on life and death alike. No tears came in her eyes and the quiver had left her lips. She gazed at him calmly, trying perhaps to read the riddle of his smile. And all the while Marie Delhasse looked down from under drooping lids.

I stepped up to the duchess' side. She saw me coming and turned her eyes to mine.

"He looked just like that when he asked me to marry him," she said, with the simple gravity of a child whose usual merriment is sobered by something that it cannot understand.

I doubted not that he had. Life, marriage, death--so he had faced them all, with scorn and weariness and acquiescence--all, save that one passion which bore him beyond himself.

The duchess spread the handkerchief again over the dead man's face, and rose to her feet. And she looked across the dead body of the duke at Marie Delhasse. I knew not what she would say, for she must have guessed by now who the girl was that had brought her to the place. Suddenly the question came in a tone of curiosity, without resentment, yet tinctured with a delicate scorn, as though spoken across a gulf of difference:

"Did you really care for him at all?"

Marie started, but she met the duchess' eyes and answered in a low voice with a single word:

"No."

"Ah, well!" said the little duchess with a sigh; and, if I read aright what she expressed, it was a pitying recognition of the reason in that answer: he could not have expected anyone to love him, she seemed to say. And if that were so, then indeed had the finger of truth guided the duke in the penning of his epitaph.

We three, who were standing round the body, seemed sunk in our own thoughts, and it was Gustave de Berensac who went to the servant and bade him bring the carriage nearer to where we were; and when it was come, they two lifted the duke in and disposed his body as well as they could. The man mounted the box, and at a foot-pace we set out. The duchess had not spoken again, nor had Marie Delhasse; but when I took my place by Marie the duchess suffered Gustave to join her, and in this order we passed along. But before we had gone far, when indeed we had but just reached the road, we met four of the police hurrying along; and before they came to us or saw what was in the carriage, one cried:

"Have you seen a small spare man pass this way lately? He would be running perhaps, or walking fast."

I stepped forward and drew them aside, signing the carriage to go on and to the others to follow it.

"I can tell you all there is to be told about him, if you mean the man whom I think you mean," said I. "But I doubt if you will catch him now."

And with that I told them the story briefly, and so far as it affected the matter they were engaged upon; and they heard it with much astonishment. For they had tracked Pierre (or Raymond Pinceau as they called him, saying it was his true name) to Bontet's stable, on the matter of the previous attempt on the necklace and the death of Lafleur, and on no other, and did not think to hear such a sequel as I unfolded to them.

"And if you will search," said I, "some six yards behind the wall, and maybe a quarter of a mile from the road, I fancy you will find Bontet; he may have crawled a little way, but could not far, I think. As for the Duke of Saint-Maclou, gentlemen, his body was in the carriage that passed you this moment. And I am at your service, although I would desire, if it be possible, to be allowed to follow my friends."

There being but four of them and their anxiety being to achieve the capture of Pierre, they made no difficulty of allowing me to go on my way, taking from me my promise to present myself before the magistrate at Avranches next day; and leaving two to seek for Bontet, the other two made on, in the hope of finding a boat to take them to the Mount, whither they conceived the escaped man must have directed his steps.

Thus delayed, I was some time behind the others in reaching the inn, and I found Gustave waiting for me in the entrance. The body of the duke had been carried to his own room and a messenger sent to procure a proper conveyance. Marie Delhasse was upstairs, and Gustave's message to me was that the duchess desired to see me.

"Nay," said I, "there is one thing I want to do before that;" and I called to a servant girl who was hovering between terror and excitement at the events of the evening, and asked her whether Mme. Delhasse had returned.

"No, sir," she answered. "The lady left word that she would be back in half an hour, but she has not yet returned."

Then I said to Gustave de Berensac, laying my hand on his shoulder:

"When I am married, Gustave, you will not meet my mother-in-law in my house;" and I left Gustave staring in an amazement not unnatural to his ignorance. And I allowed myself to be directed by the servant girl to where the duchess sat.

The duchess waited till the door was shut, and then turned to me as if about to speak, but I was beforehand with her; and I began:

"Forgive me for speaking of the necklace, but I fear it is still missing."

The duchess looked at me scornfully.

"He gave it to the girl again, I suppose?" she asked.

"He gave it," I answered, "to the girl's mother, and she, I fear, has made off with it;" and I told the duchess how Mme. Delhasse had laid her plot. The duchess heard me in silence, but at the end she remarked:

"It does not matter. I would never have worn the thing again; but it was a pretty plot between them."

"The duke had no thought," I began, "but that--"

"Oh, I meant between mother and daughter," said the duchess. "The mother gets the diamonds from my husband; the daughter, it seems, Mr. Aycon, is likely to get respectability from you; and I suppose they will share the respective benefits when this trouble has blown over."

It was no use to be angry with her; to confess the truth, I felt that anger would come ill from me. So I did but say very quietly:

"I think you are wrong. Mlle. Delhasse knew nothing of her mother's device."

"You do not deny all of what I say," observed the duchess.

"Mlle. Delhasse," I returned, "is in no need of what you suggest; but I hope that she will be my wife."

"And some day," said the duchess, "you will see the necklace--or perhaps that would not be safe. Madame will send the money."

"When it happens," said I, "on my honor, I will write and tell you."

The duchess, with a toss of her head which meant "Well, I'm right and you're wrong," rose from her seat.

"I must take poor Armand home," said she. "M. de Berensac is going with me. Will you accompany us?"

"If you will give me a delay of one hour, I will most willingly."

"What have you to do in that hour, Mr. Aycon?"

"I purpose to escort Mlle. Delhasse back to the convent and leave her there. I suppose we shall all have to answer some questions in regard to this sad matter, and where can she stay near Avranches save there?"

"She certainly can't come to my house," said the duchess.

"It would be impossible under the circumstances," I agreed.

"Under any circumstances," said the duchess haughtily.

By this time a covered conveyance had been procured, and when the duchess, having fired her last scornful remark at me, walked to the door of the inn, the body of the duke was being placed in it. Gustave de Berensac assisted the servant, and their task was just accomplished when Jacques Bontet was carried by two of the police to the door. The man was alive and would recover, they said, and be able to stand his trial. But as yet no news had come of the fortune that attended the pursuit of Raymond Pinceau, otherwise known as Pierre. It was conjectured that he must have had a boat waiting for him at or near the Mount, and, gaining it, had for the moment at least made good his escape.

"But we shall find about that from Bontet," said one of them, with a complacent nod at the fellow who lay still in a sort of stupor, with blood-stained bandages round his head.

I stood by the door of the duchess' carriage, in which she and Gustave were to follow the body of the duke, and when she came to step in I offered her my hand. But she would have none of it. She got in unassisted, and Gustave followed her. They were about to move off, when suddenly, running from the house in wild dismay, came Marie Delhasse, and caring for none of those who stood round, she seized my arm, crying:

"My mother is neither in the sitting room nor in her bedroom! Where is she?"

Now I saw no need to tell Marie at that time what had become of Mme. Delhasse. The matter, however, was not left in my hands; no, nor in those of Gustave de Berensac, who called out hastily to the driver, "Ready! Go on, go on!" The duchess called "Wait!" and then she turned to Marie Delhasse and said in calm cold tones:

"You ask where your mother is. Well, then, where is the necklace?"

Marie drew back as though she had been struck; yet her grip did not leave my arm, but tightened on it.

"The necklace?" she gasped.

And the duchess, using the most scornful words she knew and giving a short little laugh, said.

"Your mother has levanted with the necklace. Of course you didn't know!"

Thus, if Marie Delhasse had been stern to the Duke of Saint-Maclou when he lay dying, his wife avenged him to the full and more. For at the words, at the sight of the duchess' disdainful face and of my troubled look, Marie uttered a cry and reeled and sank half-fainting in my arms.

"Oh, drive on!" said the Duchess of Saint-Maclou in a wearied tone.

And away they drove, leaving us two alone. Nor did Marie speak again, unless it were in distressed incoherent protests, till, an hour later, I delivered her into the charge of the Mother Superior at the convent by the side of the bay. And the old lady bade me wait till she saw Marie comfortably bestowed, and then she returned to me and we walked side by side for a while in the little burying-ground, she listening to an outline of my story. Perhaps I, in a lover's zeal, spoke harshly of the duchess; for the old lady put her hand upon my arm and said to me:

"It was not for losing the diamonds that her heart was sore--poor silly child!"

And, inasmuch as I doubted whether my venerable friend thought that it was for the loss of her husband either, I held my peace.

CHAPTER XXII.
From Shadow to Sunshine.

There remains yet one strange and terrible episode of which I must tell, though indeed, I thank God, I was in no way a witness of it. A week after the events which I have set down, while Marie still lay prostrate at the convent, and I abode at my old hotel in Avranches, assisting to the best of my power in the inquiry being held by the local magistrate, an officer of police arrived from Havre; and when the magistrate had heard his story, he summoned me from the ante-room where I was waiting, and bade me also listen to the story. And this it was:

At the office where tickets were taken for a ship on the point to make the voyage to America, among all the crowd about to cross, it chanced that two people met one another--an elderly woman whose face was covered by a thick veil, and a short spare man who wore a fair wig and large red whiskers. Yet, notwithstanding these disguises, the pair knew one another. For at first sight of the woman, the man cowered away and tried to hide himself; while she, perceiving him, gave a sudden scream and clutched eagerly at the pocket of her dress.

Seeing himself feared, the ruffian took courage, his quick brain telling him that the woman also was seeking to avoid recognition. And when she had taken her ticket, he contrived to see the book and, finding a name which he did not know as hers, he tracked her to the inn where she was lodging till the vessel should start. When he walked into the inn, she shrank before him and turned pale--for he caught her with the veil off her face--and again she clutched at her pocket. He sat down near her: for a while she sat still; then she rose and walked out into the air, as though she went for a walk. But he, suspecting rightly that she would not return, tracked her again to another inn, meaner and more obscure than the first, and, walking in, he sat down by her. And again the third time this was done: and there were people who had been at each of the inns to speak to it: and those at the third inn said that the woman looked as though Satan himself had taken his place by her--so full of helplessness and horror was she; while the man smiled under alert bright eyes that would not leave her face, except now and again for a swift watchful glance round the room. For he was now hunter and hunted both; yet, like a dog that will be slain rather than loose his hold, he chose to risk his own life, if by that he might not lose sight of the unhappy woman. Two lives had been spent already in the quest: a third was nought to him; and the woman's air and clutching of her pocket had set an idea afloat in his brain. The vessel was to sail at six the next morning; and it was eight in the evening when the man sat down opposite the woman in the third inn they visited--it was no better than a drinking shop near the quays. For half an hour they sat, and there was that in their air that made them observed. Suddenly the man crossed over to the woman and whispered in her ear. She started, crying low yet audibly, "You lie!" But he spoke to her again; and then she rose and paid her score and walked out of the inn on to the quays, followed by her unrelenting attendant. It was dark now, or quite dusk; and a loiterer at the door distinguished their figures among the passing crowd but for a few yards: then they disappeared; and none was found who had seen them again, either under cover or in the open air, that night.

And for my part, I like not to think how the night passed for that wretched old woman; for at some hour and in some place, near by the water, the man found her alone, and ran his prey to the ground before the bloodhounds that were on his track could come up with them.

Indeed he almost won safety, or at least respite; for the ship was already mov-ing when she was boarded by the police, who, searching high and low, came at last on the spare man with the red whiskers; these an officer rudely plucked off and the fair wig with them, and called the prisoner by the name of Pinceau. The little man made one rush with a knife, and, foiled in that, another for the side of the vessel. But his efforts were useless. He was handcuffed and led on shore. And when he was searched, the stones which had gone to compose the great treasure of the family of Saint-Maclou--the Cardinal's Necklace--were found hidden here and there about him; but the setting was gone.

And the woman? Let me say it briefly. Great were her sins, and not the greatest of them was the theft of the Cardinal's Necklace. Yet the greater that she took in hand to do was happily thwarted; and I pray that she found mercy when the deep dark waters of the harbor swallowed her on that night, and gave back her body to a shameful burial.

*   *   *   *   *

In the quiet convent by the shores of the bay the wind of the world, with its burden of sin and sorrow, blows faintly and with tempered force: the talk of idle, eager tongues cannot break across the comforting of kind voices and the sweet strains of quiet worship. Raymond Pinceau was dead, and Jacques Bontet condemned to lifelong penal servitude; and the world had ceased to talk of the story that had been revealed at the trial of these men, and--what the world loved even more to discuss--of how much of the story had not been revealed.

For although M. de Vieuville, President of the Court which tried Bontet, and father of Alfred de Vieuville, that friend of the duke's who was to have acted at the duel, complimented me on the candor with which I gave my evidence, yet he did not press me beyond what was strictly necessary to bring home to the prisoners the crimes of murder and attempted robbery with which they were charged. Not till I knew the Judge, having been introduced to him by his son, did he ask me further of the matter; and then, sitting on the lawn of his country-house, I told him the whole story, as it has been set down in this narrative, saving only sundry matters which had passed between the duchess and myself on the one hand, and between Marie Delhasse and myself on the other. Yet I do not think that my reticence availed me much against an acumen trained and developed by dialectic struggles with generations of criminals. For the first question which M. de Vieuville put to me was this:

"And what of the girl, Mr. Aycon? She has suffered indeed for the sins of others."

But young Alfred, who was standing by, laid a hand on his father's shoulder and said with a laugh:

"Father, when Mr. Aycon leaves us tomorrow, it is to visit the convent at Avranches." And the old man held out his hand to me, saying:

"You do well."

To the convent at Avranches then I went one bright morning in the spring of the next year; and again I walked with the stately old lady in the little burial ground. Yet she was a little less stately, and I thought that there was what the profane might call a twinkle in her eye, as she deplored Marie's disinclination to become a permanent inmate of the establishment over which she presided. And on her lips came an indubitable smile when I leaped back from her in horror at the thought.

"There would be none here to throw her troubles in her teeth," pursued the Mother Superior, smiling still. "None to remind her of her mother's shame; none to lay snares for her; none to remind her of the beauty which has brought so much woe on her; no men to disturb her life with their angry conflicting passions. Does not the picture attract you, Mr. Aycon?"

"As a picture," said I, "it is almost perfect. There is but one blemish in it."

"A blemish? I do not perceive it."

"Why, madame, I cannot find anywhere in your canvas the figure of myself."

With a laugh she turned away and passed through the arched gateway. And I saw my friend, the little nun who had first opened the door to me when I came seeking the duchess, pass by and pause a moment to look at me. Then I was left alone till Marie came to me through the gateway: and I sprang up to meet her.

I have been candid throughout, and I will be candid now--even though my plain speaking strikes not at myself, but at Marie, who must forgive me as best she may. For I believe she meant to marry me from the very first; and I doubt whether if I had taken the dismissal she gave, I should have been allowed to go far on my solitary way. Indeed I think she did but want to hear me say how that all she urged was lighter than a feather against my love for her, and, if that were her desire, she was gratified to the full; seeing that for a moment she frightened me, and I outdid every lover since the world began (it cannot be that I deceive myself in thinking that) in vehemence and insistence. So that she reproved me, adding:

"You can hardly speak the truth in all that you say: for at first, you know, you were more than half in love with the Duchess of Saint-Maclou."

For a moment I was silenced. Then I looked at Marie: and I found in her words no more a rebuke, but a provocation--aye, a challenge to prove that by no possibility could I, who loved her so passionately, ever have been so much as half in love with any woman in the whole world, the Duchess of Saint-Maclou not excepted.

And prove it I did that morning in the burial ground of the convent, to my own complete satisfaction, and thereby overcame the last doubts which afflicted Marie Delhasse.

And if, in spite of that most exhaustive and satisfactory proof, the thing proved remained not much more true than the thing disproved--why, it is not my fault. For Love has a virtue of oblivion--yes, and a better still: that which is past he, exceeding in power all Olympus besides, makes as though it had never been, never could have been, and was from the first entirely impossible, absurd, and inconceivable. And for an instance of what I say--if indeed a further example than my own be needed, which should not be the case--let us look at the Duchess of Saint-Maclou herself.

For, if I were half in love with the duchess, which I by no means admit, modesty shall not blind me from holding that the duchess was as good a half in love with me. Yet, when I had been married to Marie Delhasse some six months, I received a letter from my good friend Gustave de Berensac, informing me of his approaching union with Mme. de Saint-Maclou. And, if I might judge from Gustave's letter, he repudiated utterly the idea which I have ventured to suggest concerning the duchess.

Two other facts Gustave mentioned--both of them, I think, with a touch of apology. The first was that the duchess, being unable to endure the horrible associations now indissolubly connected with the Cardinal's Necklace, of which she had become owner for the term of her life--

"What? Won't she wear it?" asked my wife at this point: she was (as wives will) leaning over my shoulder as I read the letter.

It was what I also had expected to read; but what I did read was that the duchess, ingeniously contriving to save both her feelings and her diamonds, had caused the stones to be set in a tiara--"which," continued Gustave (I am sure he was much in love) "will not have any of the unpleasant associations connected with the necklace."

And the second fact? It was this--just this, though it was wrapped up in all the roundabout phrases and softened by all the polite expressions of friendship of which Gustave was master,--yet just this,--that he was not in a position to invite myself and my wife to the wedding! For the little duchess, consistent to the end, in spite of his entreaties and protests, had resolutely and entirely declined to receive

Mrs. Aycon!

I finished the letter and looked up at Marie. And Marie, looking thoughtfully down at the paper, observed:

"I always told you that she was fond of you, you know."

But, for my part, I hope that Marie's explanation is not the true one. I prefer to attribute the duchess' refusal--in which, I may state, she steadily persists--to some mistaken and misplaced sense of propriety; or, if that fails me, then I will set it down to the fact that Marie's presence would recall too many painful and distressing scenes, and be too full of unpleasant associations. Thus understood, the duchess' refusal was quite natural and agreed completely with what she had done in respect of the necklace--for it was out of the question to turn the edge of the difficulty by converting Marie into a tiara!

So the duchess will not receive my wife. But I forgive her--for, beyond doubt, but for the little duchess and that indiscretion of hers, I should not have received my wife myself!

The Codes Of Hammurabi And Moses
W. W. Davies

QTY

The discovery of the Hammurabi Code is one of the greatest achievements of archaeology, and is of paramount interest, not only to the student of the Bible, but also to all those interested in ancient history...

Religion   **ISBN: *1-59462-338-4***   **Pages:132**

MSRP $12.95

The Theory of Moral Sentiments
Adam Smith

QTY

This work from 1749. contains original theories of conscience amd moral judgment and it is the foundation for systemof morals.

Philosophy ISBN: *1-59462-777-0*   **Pages:536**

MSRP $19.95

Jessica's First Prayer
Hesba Stretton

QTY

In a screened and secluded corner of one of the many railway-bridges which span the streets of London there could be seen a few years ago, from five o'clock every morning until half past eight, a tidily set-out coffee-stall, consisting of a trestle and board, upon which stood two large tin cans, with a small fire of charcoal burning under each so as to keep the coffee boiling during the early hours of the morning when the work-people were thronging into the city on their way to their daily toil...

Pages:84

Childrens   ISBN: *1-59462-373-2*   *MSRP $9.95*

My Life and Work
Henry Ford

QTY

Henry Ford revolutionized the world with his implementation of mass production for the Model T automobile. Gain valuable business insight into his life and work with his own auto-biography... "We have only started on our development of our country we have not as yet, with all our talk of wonderful progress, done more than scratch the surface. The progress has been wonderful enough but..."

Pages:300

Biographies/   ISBN: *1-59462-198-5*   *MSRP $21.95*

The Art of Cross-Examination
Francis Wellman

QTY

I presume it is the experience of every author, after his first book is published upon an important subject, to be almost overwhelmed with a wealth of ideas and illustrations which could readily have been included in his book, and which to his own mind, at least, seem to make a second edition inevitable. Such certainly was the case with me; and when the first edition had reached its sixth impression in five months, I rejoiced to learn that it seemed to my publishers that the book had met with a sufficiently favorable reception to justify a second and considerably enlarged edition. ..

Reference   ISBN: *1-59462-647-2*

Pages:412

MSRP $19.95

On the Duty of Civil Disobedience
Henry David Thoreau

QTY

Thoreau wrote his famous essay, On the Duty of Civil Disobedience, as a protest against an unjust but popular war and the immoral but popular institution of slave-owning. He did more than write—he declined to pay his taxes, and was hauled off to gaol in consequence. Who can say how much this refusal of his hastened the end of the war and of slavery ?

Law   ISBN: *1-59462-747-9*

Pages:48

MSRP $7.45

Dream Psychology Psychoanalysis for Beginners
Sigmund Freud

QTY

Sigmund Freud, born Sigismund Schlomo Freud (May 6, 1856 - September 23, 1939), was a Jewish-Austrian neurologist and psychiatrist who co-founded the psychoanalytic school of psychology. Freud is best known for his theories of the unconscious mind, especially involving the mechanism of repression; his redefinition of sexual desire as mobile and directed towards a wide variety of objects; and his therapeutic techniques, especially his understanding of transference in the therapeutic relationship and the presumed value of dreams as sources of insight into unconscious desires.

Psychology   ISBN: *1-59462-905-6*

Pages:196

MSRP $15.45

The Miracle of Right Thought
Orison Swett Marden

QTY

Believe with all of your heart that you will do what you were made to do. When the mind has once formed the habit of holding cheerful, happy, prosperous pictures, it will not be easy to form the opposite habit. It does not matter how improbable or how far away this realization may see, or how dark the prospects may be, if we visualize them as best we can, as vividly as possible, hold tenaciously to them and vigorously struggle to attain them, they will gradually become actualized, realized in the life. But a desire, a longing without endeavor, a yearning abandoned or held indifferently will vanish without realization.

Pages:360

Self Help   ISBN: *1-59462-644-8*

MSRP $25.45

The Rosicrucian Cosmo-Conception Mystic Christianity by *Max Heindel*   ISBN: *1-59462-188-8*   **$38.95**
The Rosicrucian Cosmo-conception is not dogmatic, neither does it appeal to any other authority than the reason of the student. It is: not controversial, but is: sent forth in the, hope that it may help to clear...   New Age/Religion Pages 646

Abandonment To Divine Providence by *Jean-Pierre de Caussade*   ISBN: *1-59462-228-0*   **$25.95**
"The Rev. Jean Pierre de Caussade was one of the most remarkable spiritual writers of the Society of Jesus in France in the 18th Century. His death took place at Toulouse in 1751. His works have gone through many editions and have been republished...   Inspirational/Religion Pages 400

Mental Chemistry by *Charles Haanel*   ISBN: *1-59462-192-6*   **$23.95**
Mental Chemistry allows the change of material conditions by combining and appropriately utilizing the power of the mind. Much like applied chemistry creates something new and unique out of careful combinations of chemicals the mastery of mental chemistry...   New Age Pages 354

The Letters of Robert Browning and Elizabeth Barret Barrett 1845-1846 vol II   ISBN: *1-59462-193-4*   **$35.95**
by *Robert Browning* and *Elizabeth Barrett*   Biographies Pages 596

Gleanings In Genesis (volume I) by *Arthur W. Pink*   ISBN: *1-59462-130-6*   **$27.45**
Appropriately has Genesis been termed "the seed plot of the Bible" for in it we have, in germ form, almost all of the great doctrines which are afterwards fully developed in the books of Scripture which follow...   Religion/Inspirational Pages 420

The Master Key by *L. W. de Laurence*   ISBN: *1-59462-001-6*   **$30.95**
In no branch of human knowledge has there been a more lively increase of the spirit of research during the past few years than in the study of Psychology, Concentration and Mental Discipline. The requests for authentic lessons in Thought Control, Mental Discipline and...   New Age/Business Pages 422

The Lesser Key Of Solomon Goetia by *L. W. de Laurence*   ISBN: *1-59462-092-X*   **$9.95**
This translation of the first book of the "Lemegton" which is now for the first time made accessible to students of Talismanic Magic was done, after careful collation and edition, from numerous Ancient Manuscripts in Hebrew, Latin, and French...   New Age/Occult Pages 92

Rubaiyat Of Omar Khayyam by *Edward Fitzgerald*   ISBN:*1-59462-332-5*   **$13.95**
Edward Fitzgerald, whom the world has already learned, in spite of his own efforts to remain within the shadow of anonymity, to look upon as one of the rarest poets of the century, was born at Bredfield, in Suffolk, on the 31st of March, 1809. He was the third son of John Purcell...   Music Pages 172

Ancient Law by *Henry Maine*   ISBN: *1-59462-128-4*   **$29.95**
The chief object of the following pages is to indicate some of the earliest ideas of mankind, as they are reflected in Ancient Law, and to point out the relation of those ideas to modern thought.   Religion/History Pages 452

Far-Away Stories by *William J. Locke*   ISBN: *1-59462-129-2*   **$19.45**
"Good wine needs no bush, but a collection of mixed vintages does. And this book is just such a collection. Some of the stories I do not want to remain buried for ever in the museum files of dead magazine-numbers an author's not unpardonable vanity..."   Fiction Pages 272

Life of David Crockett by *David Crockett*   ISBN: *1-59462-250-7*   **$27.45**
"Colonel David Crockett was one of the most remarkable men of the times in which he lived. Born in humble life, but gifted with a strong will, an indomitable courage, and unremitting perseverance...   Biographies/New Age Pages 424

Lip-Reading by *Edward Nitchie*   ISBN: *1-59462-206-X*   **$25.95**
Edward B. Nitchie, founder of the New York School for the Hard of Hearing, now the Nitchie School of Lip-Reading, Inc, wrote "LIP-READING Principles and Practice". The development and perfecting of this meritorious work on lip-reading was an undertaking...   How-to Pages 400

A Handbook of Suggestive Therapeutics, Applied Hypnotism, Psychic Science   ISBN: *1-59462-214-0*   **$24.95**
by *Henry Munro*   Health/New Age/Health/Self-help Pages 376

A Doll's House: and Two Other Plays by *Henrik Ibsen*   ISBN: *1-59462-112-8*   **$19.95**
Henrik Ibsen created this classic when in revolutionary 1848 Rome. Introducing some striking concepts in playwriting for the realist genre, this play has been studied the world over.   Fiction/Classics/Plays 308

The Light of Asia by *sir Edwin Arnold*   ISBN: *1-59462-204-3*   **$13.95**
In this poetic masterpiece, Edwin Arnold describes the life and teachings of Buddha. The man who was to become known as Buddha to the world was born as Prince Gautama of India but he rejected the worldly riches and abandoned the reigns of power when...   Religion/History/Biographies Pages 170

The Complete Works of Guy de Maupassant by *Guy de Maupassant*   ISBN: *1-59462-157-8*   **$16.95**
"For days and days, nights and nights, I had dreamed of that first kiss which was to consecrate our engagement, and I knew not on what spot I should put my lips..."   Fiction/Classics Pages 240

The Art of Cross-Examination by *Francis L. Wellman*   ISBN: *1-59462-309-0*   **$26.95**
Written by a renowned trial lawyer, Wellman imparts his experience and uses case studies to explain how to use psychology to extract desired information through questioning.   How-to/Science/Reference Pages 408

Answered or Unanswered? by *Louisa Vaughan*   ISBN: *1-59462-248-5*   **$10.95**
Miracles of Faith in China   Religion Pages 112

The Edinburgh Lectures on Mental Science (1909) by *Thomas*   ISBN: *1-59462-008-3*   **$11.95**
This book contains the substance of a course of lectures recently given by the writer in the Queen Street Hall, Edinburgh. Its purpose is to indicate the Natural Principles governing the relation between Mental Action and Material Conditions...   New Age/Psychology Pages 148

Ayesha by *H. Rider Haggard*   ISBN: *1-59462-301-5*   **$24.95**
Verily and indeed it is the unexpected that happens! Probably if there was one person upon the earth from whom the Editor of this, and of a certain previous history, did not expect to hear again...   Classics Pages 380

Ayala's Angel by *Anthony Trollope*   ISBN: *1-59462-352-X*   **$29.95**
The two girls were both pretty, but Lucy who was twenty-one who supposed to be simple and comparatively unattractive, whereas Ayala was credited, as her Bombwhat romantic name might show, with poetic charm and a taste for romance. Ayala when her father died was nineteen...   Fiction Pages 484

The American Commonwealth by *James Bryce*   ISBN: *1-59462-286-8*   **$34.45**
An interpretation of American democratic political theory. It examines political mechanics and society from the perspective of Scotsman James Bryce   Politics Pages 572

Stories of the Pilgrims by *Margaret P. Pumphrey*   ISBN: *1-59462-116-0*   **$17.95**
This book explores pilgrims religious oppression in England as well as their escape to Holland and eventual crossing to America on the Mayflower, and their early days in New England...   History Pages 268

QTY

The Fasting Cure *by Sinclair Upton*   ISBN: *1-59462-222-1*   **$13.95**
In the Cosmopolitan Magazine for May, 1910, and in the Contemporary Review (London) for April, 1910, I published an article dealing with my experiences in fasting. I have written a great many magazine articles, but never one which attracted so much attention... New Age/Self Help/Health Pages 164

Hebrew Astrology *by Sepharial*   ISBN: *1-59462-308-2*   **$13.45**
In these days of advanced thinking it is a matter of common observation that we have left many of the old landmarks behind and that we are now pressing forward to greater heights and to a wider horizon than that which represented the mind-content of our progenitors... Astrology Pages 144

Thought Vibration or The Law of Attraction in the Thought World   ISBN: *1-59462-127-6*   **$12.95**
by William Walker Atkinson   Psychology/Religion Pages 144

Optimism *by Helen Keller*   ISBN: *1-59462-108-X*   **$15.95**
Helen Keller was blind, deaf, and mute since 19 months old, yet famously learned how to overcome these handicaps, communicate with the world, and spread her lectures promoting optimism. An inspiring read for everyone... Biographies/Inspirational Pages 84

Sara Crewe *by Frances Burnett*   ISBN: *1-59462-360-0*   **$9.45**
In the first place, Miss Minchin lived in London. Her home was a large, dull, tall one, in a large, dull square, where all the houses were alike, and all the sparrows were alike, and where all the door-knockers made the same heavy sound... Childrens/Classic Pages 88

The Autobiography of Benjamin Franklin *by Benjamin Franklin*   ISBN: *1-59462-135-7*   **$24.95**
The Autobiography of Benjamin Franklin has probably been more extensively read than any other American historical work, and no other book of its kind has had such ups and downs of fortune. Franklin lived for many years in England, where he was agent... Biographies/History Pages 332

Name	
Email	
Telephone	
Address	
City, State ZIP	

☐ **Credit Card**   ☐ **Check / Money Order**

Credit Card Number	
Expiration Date	
Signature	

Please Mail to: Book Jungle
                    PO Box 2226
                    Champaign, IL 61825
     or Fax to: 630-214-0564

ORDERING INFORMATION

web*: www.bookjungle.com*
email*: sales@bookjungle.com*
fax*: 630-214-0564*
mail*: Book Jungle PO Box 2226 Champaign, IL 61825*
or PayPal *to sales@bookjungle.com*

Please contact us for bulk discounts

DIRECT-ORDER TERMS

**20% Discount if You Order
Two or More Books**
Free Domestic Shipping!
Accepted: Master Card, Visa,
Discover, American Express